THE BAD SISTER

A NOVEL

by

EMMA TENNANT

LONDON
VICTOR GOLLANCZ LTD
1978

ISBN 0 575 02493 3

The poem on page 46 is from *Marina Tsvetayeva: Selected Poems* translated by Elaine Feinstein, from a literal version by Angela Livingstone, © Oxford University Press, 1971. Reprinted by permission of Oxford University Press.

PRINTED IN GREAT BRITAIN
BY EBENEZER BAYLIS AND SON LIMITED
THE TRINITY PRESS, WORCESTER, AND LONDON

CONTENTS

Let beeves and home-bred kine partake
The sweets of Burn-mill meadow;
The swan on still St Mary's Lake
Float double, swan and shadow!

From *Yarrow Unvisited* by William Wordsworth

EDITOR'S NARRATIVE

IN THE EARLY 1950s Michael Dalzell was a young man. He owned estates in the Borders of Scotland and a small house in central London, and when he decided to marry, as we can see from this photograph, he chose as his bride a fair-haired girl of the same class as himself. The newsprint is smudged with age, but she is pretty if prim. The caption says the honeymoon would be spent abroad—but another clipping from a gossip column announces they have decided to settle immediately on their Border estates. At any rate, whether the couple went abroad or not, a daughter was conceived, and born in Scotland. A quarter of a century later both father and daughter were murdered, victims of 'political murder' at the hands of a woman who seems to have been a daughter of Dalzell. This strange case—for the killer was never found—has been the subject of many TV documentaries and journalistic 'reconstructions', but until recently the original wedding photographs, and police photographs of the corpses, and bewildered statements from friends of the family have been all the evidence available. Now, two changes have come about. Several of Dalzell's old friends have been prepared for the first time to give an account of him at about the time of his wedding, and in the course of doing so have casually mentioned 'a collection of women in the hills'; and a friend of 'Jane' (the supposed murderer) has filled in a good deal of her life before the double crime. But, most important of all, a strange document, apparently by 'Jane' herself, has come to light. It now seems possible to understand these odd killings a little better, and it may protect the health of our society if we learn to do so. They are not, after all, isolated instances —murder by middle class female urban guerillas is ever on the increase in the West—yet it is also the case that 'Jane' may not fit easily into that category of person. I will only present what I know, or have been told, and 'Jane's journal' can supply the rest.

Michael Dalzell, in the days before his troubles began, liked gambling and staying out late. This he did on July 21, 1952, on the eve of his wedding, in his London club, although he knew he would feel far from well the next day when it came to flying up for the celebrations. While the marquee was being put up at Dalzell, and a bonfire was assembled on the highest hill, the young groom and his friends sat playing backgammon and drinking champagne till dawn. The bride's name was Louise, and she was toasted from time to time, along with other women friends. At five, the future husband was half-carried into a cab, and twenty minutes later he was fumbling for the key at his door. He was not in a good temper—he even, a friend reported later, felt "rather jinxed".

The evening at the club hadn't gone well. Dalzell lost two thousand pounds, which he could only raise by sell-ing a wood on his estate, and he had the unpleasant feeling that his wife would stop him from gambling altogether once they were married. He dreaded the prospect, which Louise had also manoeuvred, of spending the rest of his life in the Borders. But most of all, in his gloomy and drunken state, he felt uneasy at the way his 'stag party' had progressed. His friends agreed they had never seen anything like it. The backgammon dice were laughingly examined, as if the points could vanish or multiply in the hands of a skilled conjuror. They couldn't, of course!— but it seemed almost unbelievable, and certainly ludicrous, that a man could play the game all night and throw nothing but twos. 'Deuce Dalzell' they began to call him by the time the brandy and champagne had been succeeded by scrambled eggs and strong coffee and followed by champagne again. "You'll be seeing double at the wedding, old boy!"

Worse was to come, though, when the young man finally negotiated his key and stepped into the house. He had left the hall and ground floor sitting room lights on, as he always did, to keep the burglars away, and even in his uncertain condition he could see that someone had turned the sitting room light off. At the same time, he saw that a shadow stretched from the half-open sitting room door onto the grey carpet of the hall. There was no grandfather clock, or similar tall piece of furniture which could have accounted for the shadow, and for a time Michael Dalzell stood stock still. It did cross his mind that tonight was as good a night to be killed as any. But, tonight at least, he was to be spared.

The girl who had climbed into the house from the rear and concealed herself in the sitting room—and whose shadow now betrayed her—had until recently been employed as shop assistant in a big London store. Her name was Mary, her mother was unmarried and Irish, and she was six months pregnant with Michael's child. Dalzell had seen her while buying white calfskin gloves for his fiancée, and had insisted she try on the gloves for him, telling her her hands were "just the right size". She had had to have them sprinkled with powder by the chief vendeuse and had rested her elbow on a velvet pad intended for customers. He bought six pairs. When the bill was signed, Mary was asked if she would like to go out later that evening, and she said she would. She certainly found him very charming, and although there were many evenings when Michael was invited to parties he wouldn't have dreamed of taking her to, they went to gambling clubs and nightclubs enough for her to feel he must be interested in her almost to the point of proposal. That this wasn't the case she discovered, inevitably, when she became pregnant. She had a difficult time, for her mother, who'd only a few years before come over from Ireland with her daughter, shocked by the news and already in poor health, working as a domestic in a big country house in Southern England, refused to see her. When she relented the mistress of the house, a Mrs Aldridge, made it clear Mary would not be welcome. Michael gave her a hundred pounds and suggested they didn't meet again. Social workers advised that the baby should be adopted. And Mary lost her job behind the glove counter when her condition became too evident. She was desperate, in fact, and having read in the gossip columns of her lover's impending marriage, decided to plead with him one last time before handing herself over to the hostel and the adoption society.

Michael Dalzell, of course, was adamant. He turned on the lights once he had come to his senses and realised who the owner of the shadow was, and he settled the girl on the sofa and poured a large brandy for each of them. He explained he had just lost two thousand pounds at backgammon and Mary found herself commiserating with him before she knew what she was doing. He said he had big expenses with his wedding, and had found it necessary to convert an upper floor at Dalzell into a nursery, which had involved the installation of central heating. He then went on to point out that the baby had the chance of a far better life if adopted, and that it was selfish of Mary to want to keep it and for him to pay for it. In the end, half-reeling from the brandy, which was new to her (whereas Michael's mind, after an evening's drinking, had been marvellously cleared by it), Mary let herself out of the house and stumbled a long way across London to the room in the shared flat she could no longer afford.

A few hours later Michael Dalzell was on the plane to the North. Events of the night before seemed already distant and unimportant. He remembered the unlucky gambling with more irritation than the episode with Mary—in fact he felt more sorry for her in retrospect than angry at her untimely visit—and it's clear that his conscience troubled him a little at the wedding, because he confided the visit to a friend and asked him to keep an eye on her in London over the next few months. By then she had moved and the friend was unable to trace her. But by then, too, Louise Dalzell was expecting a baby. By all accounts the young couple were excited and proud, and the last touches to the nursery floor had to be added in haste in order for the rooms to be ready in time for the birth.

As I was compiling these notes a letter arrived from a man named Luke Saighton, who had been a friend of Michael Dalzell in his gambling days and who had gone to stay frequently at Dalzell before the estate was sold. "I can't remember exactly when the people of whom you inquire arrived there," a part of the letter ran,

but I think it was probably the summer of 1965. I do remember one or two incidents very clearly. Michael and I were standing on the track halfway up the valley —at a point where the track divides and one part winds downwards to run a couple of miles beside the burn before petering out, and the other climbs the hill—they used it to take shooting brakes in the summer and you could get the snow plough along it in winter, for the shepherds—when we saw a car coming towards us at a terrific speed. It was only a broken-down old Austin, but the track was narrow and rough and I honestly don't know how it managed to go at such a rate. It had been a dry, dusty summer and they were in a cloud of dust—it was like a typhoon approaching. Michael and I stepped pretty quickly out of the way, as you may imagine! Anyway, when the car had gone past and we had mopped some of the dust off our faces I saw Michael was looking pretty badly shaken. I'd only just managed to get a glimpse of the inside of the car, and my first impression had been of a huddle of women, long hair and what looked like gypsy shawls and skirts. But I do remember one of the faces. She was quite young but gave us the fiercest look I've ever seen on a woman's face. It was her eyes particularly—I'm afraid I can't describe them except to say they seemed to burn right through you. "What's the matter, Michael?" I said. I really wondered if he was going to have to sit down for a while to recover himself. "It's nothing, must be the heat"—or something like it, was all he would say, but it sprang into my mind that maybe he knew the women in the car and would like his wife not to know about it. He had a bit of a reputation in the area for going after girls. (I hope, incidentally, that this will not be grossly exaggerated in your book, or documentary programme.)

Next day we heard that these women had moved into a semi-derelict cottage at the head of the valley. Michael was furious but he was very reluctant to go up there. In the end he asked me to go, and of course it was the last thing I wanted to do. If there has to be eviction I believe it is the job of the forces of law. Yet Michael didn't want to call in the police, in fact he flatly said he wouldn't. So in the end I went. It was an unpleasant business—they said they wouldn't move out —and the fierce-looking woman, who on second view wasn't as arresting as I'd thought—fairly ordinary really, medium height, brown hair, etc—was actually holding a rifle! The other woman was more pleasant, and had very white skin and dark hair and blue eyes. She spoke in a quiet voice which sounded Irish, it stood out particularly in that part of the Borders, where the Lowland Scots is very marked. She said: "We can't move, we're not going" over and over, while her friend stood behind her with the gun pointing straight at me! There was a little girl there, about twelve, she was standing with her head against the wall as if she couldn't bear the scene, so I couldn't make out what she looked like. She had dark hair, rather straggling, to her shoulders. Anyway, I told the woman I'd repeat what they'd said to Mr Dalzell, and they'd be hearing from him. "Why couldn't he come himself?" said the armed woman, with a good deal of contempt. (I couldn't help rather agreeing with her.) "No, no, leave all that out of it," the nicer-looking woman pleaded. "His time will come, Mary," was the reply. Then she turned to me and told me Mr Dalzell and I could both go to hell.

When I got back to the house I didn't repeat what the fiercer of the two women had said because I didn't want Michael to get upset again. I now think perhaps I should have. I stayed only a few days more on that occasion, and he didn't go near the place. But I was to return a month later in September for the annual shooting party, and I knew he'd have to go up there, as you

climb above that cottage to reach the butts. I did however try to make him call in the police. It seemed quite
ridiculous that he should allow these vagrants to stay
in his property. He refused again, though. I began to
suspect something, and I think Louise Dalzell did
too, so we kept off the subject.

In the event I went down with 'flu and missed the
shooting party. When I went again it was after Christmas. I remember talking to the gamekeeper about the
birds and how the September shoot had gone. I enclose
a few of his observations, and his present address, in
case you would wish to interview him.

At this point I stopped reading Luke Saighton's letter,
which had only a few more pleas, at the end of the page,
that I try not to hurt the feelings of the friends and relatives of the Dalzells, and gazed out of my study window
at the autumnal trees in the street. After collecting accounts of that summer from a few of Dalzell's old inti-
mates, it seemed fairly certain that the arrival of the women,
early 'squatters' on the laird's land, had been very annoy-
ing to him—and also, during all those months, he had
made no effort to get them out. Things only came to a
head in the spring of 1968—nearly three years after they
arrived; before the thaw, when the rain was coming
down but there was still no let-up from the cold, he sent
half a dozen farmhands up there and the women were
forced to move. It would have seemed more humane to
have done this in the summer months—yet it was certainly odd that he had allowed them to stay so long.

According to some eye-witness reports, it was because one of the women was doing her best to be aggravating that he finally evicted them. Here, as before, I can only piece together the few fragments I've been able to lay my hands on.

Michael Dalzell, after his marriage, soon settled down to become a typical landlord of those parts: Tory-voting, suspicious of change, and with a television kept in a back pantry, seldom visited either by himself or his wife. Louise Dalzell was a perfect complement to him and was popular in the village, in this neutralising much of the hostility which inevitably built up for her lazy and wealthy husband. The daughter born to them was to prove an only child and both parents adored her. By the mid-sixties, when she was twelve years old, Michael and Louise, despite social changes more marked then in England than in Scotland, were planning her London début, followed by some years in a foreign university, and her eventual takeover, for death duty reasons, of the Dalzell estate. The arrival of the women in the valley, however, caused a certain strain between husband and wife, which was reflected in a rather maddening 'hoity-toity' manner in the child—and this manner was made worse by the daily conflict, at the village school, between the daughter of the Dalzells and the girl, the same age as herself, from the half-ruined cottage in the hills. They fought so often and so angrily that the teacher became used to complaining to the laird. But each visit from the teacher to the 'big hoose' was followed by a visit from the fierce-looking woman from the head of the valley. In summer she walked barefoot and wore long skirts, which had never been seen at that time in the region. She and Michael Dalzell stayed in his study for a short time and when she came out it was always with the promise that he would do nothing about the situation. No-one ever knew what was said. So—going on in this way—the strains began to show in the Dalzell family. It was as if a shadow had fallen over the happy household—this was the opinion of others as well as Luke Saighton.

These weren't the only troubles. Michael Dalzell, bored perhaps with rural life, and uneasy at home, began to gamble again. He took to meeting friends at the Black Barony, a remote hotel in East Lothian, and playing championships and drinking all night in rented rooms. It was at this hotel in fact that he gave a dance for his daughter in the New Year of 1968, and at the dance that the incident occurred which led to the expulsion of the illegal ménage from the Dalzell estates. But before we return to Luke Saighton's account of the party, it's worth quoting from the gamekeeper (not a man to have been on the side of the squatters, of course), and to record that Michael Dalzell started to sell portions of his land to meet his gambling debts, keeping this secret from his wife and usual lawyers by using a small firm of Edinburgh solicitors. He must have been in a fairly desperate frame of mind, for however hard he tried to prevent the modern world from coming into his kingdom, it came: a woman reporter from London appeared one day and said she had heard there was a 'commune of radical feminists' up in the hills beyond his house and she was going to write about them; several more women *did* arrive in the summer of '67, and Michael Dalzell could only look the other way; and there were reports of Revolution on all sides. Not that these factors in any way disturbed the Dalzell capital or landholdings—it seemed more that he was intent, at this historically suitable time, on losing all his possessions himself. The gaming table was the most aristocratic and honourable method and the laird applied himself to the partitions of the backgammon board with more zeal than had been allotted to his fields.

It can't have been pleasant for Michael, or his wife and daughter, to go out on a country walk in those days. Possibly, in his difficult situation—for as well as his backgammon losses Dalzell must surely have also been regularly blackmailed by the women in the cottage—he cared less about the gradual loss of his land now that it was no place to be quiet and private in. For, according to Mac-Donald the gamekeeper, wherever they went a contingent of women followed. There was a small shop in the village, where Mrs Dalzell bought wool, and her daughter, now fifteen, went to look at the women's magazines; here mother and daughter would find themselves surrounded, in a place that was by no means large, by women in long black skirts and with scarves tied around their heads. The atmosphere soon became intensely claustrophobic, and the lady and her daughter had to leave. The villagers thought this shocking, but when it came to speaking openly to the women, something seemed to prevent them. MacDonald, who had no such scruples, was often shouting to them to get off the land—they disturbed the phea-

sants' feeding—and on one occasion suggested to Michael
Dalzell that he "take a shot or two, just wing them, sir,"
but at this his employer only shook his head. As Mac-
Donald pointed out to Luke Saighton, Mr Dalzell was
"too kind-hearted. Wherever he went, and the ladies
too, over the moor or along the brae, they followed
behind like a row of corbies." Certainly it seems these
women had the upper hand at that time, and that they
almost invited the pitched battle with the farmhands
which was the result of the party at the Black Barony
Hotel.

Luke Saighton's account runs:

I don't know why Michael chose to give the dance for
his daughter at a hotel rather than at home. I don't
want to be 'psychological' about it but I think holding
the party at Dalzell might have given him painful
memories of his own wedding party, when everything
seemed to be set fair, and it was glorious weather too
with the light fading almost at midnight and a bonfire
on the hill. He seemed deliberately to choose mid-
winter and another setting—on the other hand I gather
he was in debt to the Black Barony and had promised
to bring them a lot of publicity (they thought Michael
was the friend of kings and multi-millionaires). The
proprietors of the Black Barony must have been horribly disappointed when, uninvited of course, the
party from the derelict camp arrived. I gather they
thought Mr Dalzell had decided on a fancy dress occasion when they saw the gypsy attire—one or two

neighbouring landholders went home to deck themselves out with plaids and mantillas before returning to the dance. At any rate, they let them in—and then there was the devil to pay.

Michael and Louise's daughter was looking particularly pretty that night. She had fair, curly hair tied up on the top of her head if I remember, and a new dress she was very proud of. All the young men wanted to dance with her, and there was quite a crowd round her most of the time. There were Scottish reels and a few ordinary dances—even at that time Michael wasn't going to have any 'pop' or rock and roll or whatever you call it. And it was in the middle of the 'Wee Drops of Brandy' which had always been a family favourite at Dalzell before the bad luck set in, that the 'corbies' walked straight across the dance floor and went for the girl. Just like that. The fierce-looking one —I heard the quiet one called Mary crying her name as they went into the fray—was called Margaret. There were two others, whose names I didn't catch, and there was the black-haired girl who was the daughter of Mary. It was extremely shocking to see their violence. Margaret had pulled the poor girl's dress off—and someone had lurched into a waiter carrying a tray of fruit cup, so that she was covered in slices of peach and raspberries and so on. Mary's daughter looked as if she was honestly trying to scratch her eyes out. And the others were all kicking and punching. When Louise Dalzell came running up they gave her the same treatment. It took about fifteen men to pull the women off.

All the while the Scottish dance music went on because the band was in an alcove and couldn't see what was happening. I must say I shall never forget that evening. I needn't describe Michael's reactions. He was as white as a sheet, and although one shouldn't joke about a late friend, if anyone had had a few too many 'wee drops', he had. Frankly, he was quite incapable of coping with the onslaught. I think he knew if he came forward they'd go for him too—and he'd go down with the first blow.

He got his revenge the next day, of course. An army of farmhands went up the valley to the cottage—they had sticks, and two of them were allowed to take guns —not MacDonald the gamekeeper, as he might have proved too keen—and in an hour the battle was over and the women were loaded onto a farm lorry and driven to the border. Michael wanted me to go up there and help with the eviction, but I really didn't have the stomach for it. And he was keen, too, for them to be deposited in England—I don't know why—perhaps he felt they'd be further away if they were in another country. I can't remember where they were dropped off, but it was somewhere south of Carlisle.

There was one odd thing about that day. Michael told me that when it came to loading the women onto the lorry there was no sign of Margaret anywhere. Departure was held up for a good time while they searched for her. Everyone knew she was the most dangerous of the lot, and well capable of going to ground and building up a new centre on another part of the Dalzell estate. But she had completely vanished. Mary'd obviously tried to go with her, but she didn't get far. They found her in a snow drift, in a deep cleuch below the cottage. They bundled her onto the lorry and some of the men, I believe, took trouble to wrap her in her shawls. She had a poor physique apparently, could never have lasted the course. Anyway, the other women swore Meg had left the night before, after the fight, cutting across country to the Yarrow, on to Moffat and then south. As Michael still refused point blank to call in the police, there was no way of making roadblocks and catching her there: it wouldn't have been easy anyway, with those great stretches of hill and heather, and the dwarf forests of pine trees as far as the eye can see. Two reports came in the following day—one that a distant figure, probably a woman (it had long hair, but then this was 1968 and so did many men), was seen running amongst the trees on a steep hillside near St Mary's Loch. It "flitted like a shadow in the trees," the onlooker said, "zigzagging backwards and forwards as if it had no idea of direction". The other report was of a polite, well-dressed woman, never seen in the neighbourhood before, who walked up the drive at Dalzell, met Louise Dalzell walking there, exchanged a few words with her, saying she was going to visit relatives in the village, and then, when Mrs Dalzell turned round to take another glimpse of her, had disappeared. When asked what this mysterious stranger had looked like, Mrs Dalzell—who was still suffering from shock from the night before—said only that she was "quite sure she had seen her somewhere before". No, not last night, but the face was very familiar to her. She even felt it might be some distant relative of *hers* who, coming on her suddenly in the drive, was too embarrassed to declare herself. Well, of the two reports we could make nothing much. With the first, Michael and I concluded the running figure must have been a roedeer. There are a few left in the region, and particularly in the old trees of what was once the Ettrick Forest, which was where the report came from (not so far across country from the 'commune' but it seems fairly unlikely Margaret would have run off in this way). With the second, we put Louise's 'hallucination' down to shock. We made a few inquiries in the village, and in fact no-one had received a visitor that day. I wondered if she should see a doctor, but again Michael was adamant that no-one from outside should interfere in this matter. A day later, I left. When I next saw Michael and Louise—when they had moved to London—the subject didn't come up, and I'd pretty well forgotten it too. I would of course be very grateful if you could let me know any developments that may crop up in your investigations. I feel, as I am sure you do, that the police have been very inefficient in this matter: surely this 'daughter' of Michael's, if this is what she really is, can't be impossible to trace. After the death of Michael and his daughter, I felt I should have given more information on the subject of the invasion of the women during those years, but at the time, as you must understand, I couldn't see there could possibly be any connection between those women and the killings, and I was particularly anxious not to hurt Louise's relatives by dragging in even the shadow of a doubt of Michael's devotion and fidelity as a husband. I look forward to hearing from you if there are any developments.

I couldn't help thinking, when I'd read this letter, that Luke Saighton should certainly have told the police about the commune of women in the hills. But perhaps he was as shocked and disbelieving as Michael Dalzell: to them it seemed incredible that a humble, pregnant shopgirl, the classic recipient of a cash hand-out and abandonment, should in the course of twelve years have become an aggressive member of a large and growing aggressive army. If this was the present, they didn't want to know about it. They simply shut their eyes and ears.

Michael Dalzell sold his estate in 1970, to pay his gambling debts. His wife wasn't given the reason, and was simply told by her husband that he thought it was time they went back to London so he could 'go into the City'. He would have been quite unable to do this, of course, or to support his family, if a stroke of luck hadn't befallen him in the form of the deaths of two uncles and the unexpected inheritance of a large fortune from the other branch of the Dalzell family. If the twos he had thrown at backgammon seventeen years before had brought him bad luck, lasting all that time, now things seemed to have reversed very favourably: within three months of the sale of house and land, Michael Dalzell and his wife and

28

daughter were esconced in a magnificent house in Hampstead. Plans were immediately under way for a ball—in the photograph here, taken from the society pages of a glossy magazine, all three, as they stand shaking hands in the reception line, look as happy and prosperous as might be expected.

As I said earlier, there would have been little point in recapping the story of the Dalzells, if it hadn't been for Stephen, the young man who came forward in reply to my latest batch of advertisements. His evidence, and the document we print here which is the journal of the mysterious 'Jane', have solidified the picture considerably —have made it possible, indeed, to reconstruct, as we have just done, Michael Dalzell's early escapade in London. But, until the girl is found, nothing can be certain.

Stephen came to my study one morning with a copy of the *Times*—my advertisement appeared in the Personal Columns that day—and he seemed nervous when I offered him a chair and asked him to introduce himself. He may have thought I was a detective, I suppose, and regretted his decision to come, but I felt a certain excitement, as if I knew somehow that I was getting nearer to the truth, as soon as I saw him there.

Stephen was plump, and middle-aged and fair-haired. He wore a dog collar, and gave me the name of his parish in South London. Altogether he seemed a most unlikely companion for the killer of the Dalzells—yet, as I said, I was sure I was on the right trail at last. With some mumbling and apology, he pulled a battered-looking manuscript from his pocket and handed it to me before sitting in the armchair on the far side of my desk.

I didn't read the MS there and then. Stephen, who said he would prefer not to give his second name, explained that it had been sent to him by a woman who was a mutual friend of his and 'Jane's' and that he felt more and more convinced that 'Jane' was both the daughter and the killer of Michael Dalzell. "I don't know where Jane is," he began. (Stephen has a very soft voice and I had to lean over the desk to hear him.) "I suspect she's not alive, or she would have been found by now. But I'll tell you what I know. I met Jane first when she was about eighteen. It was at a Vietnam meeting and she was sitting next to a girl I knew slightly, who was at the LSE. We started to talk, after the meeting we had some supper, and then she took me back to meet her friends where she lived. It was a peculiar set-up. A big house in Notting Hill lived in exclusively by women. There must have been about thirty of them—there was one room on the ground floor where men were allowed to visit—quite a lot of children around, and Jane told me they all had the same surname, which was Wild. She said her mother was some-where there, and they had been in the house about three years—before that they'd been in Scotland."

I found myself giving a little grunt of satisfaction. "And did she introduce you to a woman named Margaret?" I asked in a voice as soft as Stephen's. He fiddled with his dog collar (it seemed more and more strange that he should be a friend of these Wild women, but then nowa-days one must accept new mixtures, such as radical gay clergymen or the like) and frowned before answering, more tentatively than usual: "Do you mean Meg? How could you know about *her*?"

I explained there had been a women's commune in Scotland, and the ringleader had been a fierce woman by the name of Margaret. Looking back through Luke Saighton's letter, I realised she had never been properly described, and was therefore unable to get corroboration from Stephen, except that he agreed the woman Meg was also indescribable. "I didn't meet her often, but she always seemed to look different," was how he put it. I thought for a moment of jokingly remarking that the days were long past when this changeability of appearance was known as being 'journalière'—you'd more likely get reported to the Sex Discrimination Board if you remarked on a woman's looks in this way. But I decided against it: he was of the protest generation despite his mild Church of England looks, and might decide to stop confiding in me. It was enough that this stranger had walked into my study and described what sounded very like the 'corbies', only grown in number—for he went on to say that Jane's mother was Mary, that she was Irish, and that 'Meg' was very much in control of the place.

"Did Jane ever refer to the name Dalzell then?" I asked.

"No. No, she didn't. Her name was Wild like the others, of course. But she did say she had met her father once, when her mother had taken her to his new home in London, demanding money. He wouldn't give it, but he offered to send Jane to a boarding school, which she accepted."

"A private school?"

"Yes, the commune was up in arms about it but Jane escaped and went there for a couple of years. She hated the set-up by then, I think, and wanted an ordinary . . ."

"Bourgeois," I put in, trying to keep a straight face.

"Exactly. She would have liked the childhood Michael Dalzell's legal daughter was having. Ponies, coming-out parties, everything. She was sick of the rhetoric and of being on the wrong side of the police. But in the event, the boarding school sickened her too. By the end, I mean. She found the girls limited and the teachers snobbish. So she returned to the fold. This meant that Meg's influence over her increased considerably."

"And what was that? What did she do to her?"

Stephen laughed as if he was surprised, and then gave a loud sigh.

"I'm sorry. I lived for so long worrying about what Meg would do to Jane that it's difficult to imagine that you know so much about the whole background and yet you don't know that. Well, to go back to that first meeting with Jane and the evening in the women's house, the atmosphere there was absolutely terrifying. The room I was allowed to sit in, I remember, was dark red, and although it was very much out of context, I couldn't help thinking of the front parlour of a grim Victorian brothel. While we sat and talked, several women flitted in and out, and they all had the same expression on their faces—self-contained and dedicated, eyes to the ground, like nuns but with very different, striding movements. Jane's mother brought us some coffee. She looked tired and strained, and I had the feeling she had been taken over there without knowing what she was letting herself in for, and now couldn't get out. Then Meg came in. All the women present turned to her automatically, as if waiting for orders: the strangest thing was the way they turned, though, like votaries in a temple, swinging round, eyes half-closed and then standing completely still, waiting for Meg to speak. I'll never forget it."

"And Jane?" I said, privately wondering if Stephen had gone into the Anglican Church as a reaction against all this. "Did she swing round too?"

"No. Not really. She'd been away at school until fairly recently, I suppose, and hadn't got back into the habit of complete obedience to Meg. But I could see it was Jane that Meg was most interested in. Little did I know then, of course, what she wanted her *for*."

"And did Meg give any orders?"

"Yes. Her voice was surprisingly light—almost chatty. It was her eyes that were frightening: grey and prominent and when they were fixed on you you felt it was your duty to do exactly as she said. She told them some place they were all to go to the next day—I wasn't really listening but I do have a vague memory of Islington being mentioned, and then seeing in the papers the next evening there'd been a big bank hold-up there. I wondered if it could possibly be them. The atmosphere was like that, you see, nervous and evil, with a tremendous wall of control imposed from above by Meg."

"Poor Jane," I said after a while. "Did she get away again?"

"Oh yes. She was fond of her mother, I think, and sometimes stayed for her sake. But she ran off a short while later, got a job and found a room . . ."

"What kind of job?"

"I think she started as a reporter. She went up quickly. She wrote about cinema, and in the last couple of years, before the . . . the relapse she had, she was film critic for a big magazine. Yes, she was doing well." Stephen shook his head, like a disapproving uncle. I wondered how much he *did* know, whether he had known all along that Jane had gone to kill Dalzell and then his daughter, rather than coming to the conclusion only now, on receiving the document. He must have read my thoughts then, for he leaned even further forward over my desk, and said in his soft voice: "Until I read this journal of hers, I can assure you I had no idea of what Meg was doing to Jane. I knew she had influenced her a great deal in the past, but I thought Jane was a long way from all that by then. She was living with a boyfriend too. It was tragic."

Stephen and I sat for a while in silence. He was clearly upset, remembering the gruesome events of ten years back, and I too was thinking of the evening, in March 1976, when Michael Dalzell lost his life. I opened the clippings file, and looked again at the photograph of the outside of his Hampstead house. I looked once more at a news picture of Michael Dalzell—he had grown plump and middle-aged by 1976, had taken on the features of a prosperous banker, which indeed he was—and then I flipped the photographs over until I came to the ones of him dead. There was a neat bullet wound over his left eye, which was open and round under it. He looked aggrieved and resigned at the same time. A black tie, sign that he had been at a formal dinner party, was tied very straight under his chin.

"The extraordinary thing is," Stephen said, "in this journal of hers Jane doesn't mention the affair of Mr Dalzell at all. It was the distorted version of getting the girl that made me first think . . ."

I looked up and nodded at Stephen, then went back to glancing through the clippings from the newspapers and reconstructing the night of the parricide. Michael Dalzell and his guests were half way through fillet of veal with wine and mushrooms when the butler went to answer the front door bell. Louise Dalzell, who had died a few years before, had been replaced by a succession of girl-friends, and one of these was in the hostess's chair, sipping wine and remaining quiet during the business conversation. (She announced later that she had thought of going out to answer the bell herself because she was so bored, and her decision not to had probably saved her life.) The butler returned and told Mr Dalzell that his daughter was outside, and had a gift for his birthday. She would like to give it to him personally if possible, and was sorry to come at an inconvenient hour.

Now Michael Dalzell knew it was nowhere near his birthday, but in his slight drunkenness he became easily sentimental and imagined the visitor to be his legal daughter, who lived on her own now, much to his disappointment, as he had hoped she would stay on in Hampstead and care for him after her mother's death.

He rose to his feet with a beatific smile. One of the guests said he tripped, but quickly corrected himself, on the rug by the dining room door. The next thing they heard was a shot. By the time they had run out into the hall, there was no sign of anyone—the front door was open, and Michael Dalzell was lying half in and half out—and they dragged him into the hall and closed the door (not that it would have made any difference to him), for it was a cold March night.

The butler was at first suspected of being mixed up in the Dalzell killing. He was a temporary, and therefore, having never met 'the real Miss Dalzell', could hardly be blamed for letting another woman convince him she was Dalzell's daughter. But his descriptions were very odd and contradictory and he was watched for some time, although it was obvious he would have been unable to commit the crime (after he had answered the door and called his employer, he had gone to the pantry and stayed with the parlour maid). He said at first that two women had come to the door, but one had been standing so much in the shadows behind the one who said she was Dalzell's daughter that he hadn't been able to make her out at all clearly. Then he said that as he had gone to inform the banker of the visit he had looked back and only the second woman was standing there, the first having disappeared. He described her as tall and brown-haired. When he was questioned as to why he went ahead to the dining room leaving the front door open and a total stranger standing there, there were no satisfactory answers. He only said the "gift was now in the other woman's hands" and he thought "Miss Dalzell must be behind her for some reason". That was all.

I handed Stephen the clippings and asked him if this made sense now there was a chance that it had indeed been Jane, and Meg standing in front of her. Stephen shrugged. "I don't think you were listening just now when I said it's odd there's no mention of the event in the journal. Jane could have been hypnotised, you know—either when she was there, and shooting her father, or afterwards into forgetting she had been there at all. God knows what new powers Meg had over her by then."

"But you didn't know that Jane had been seeing Meg again? And what 'powers' do you mean?" (I was conscious of feeling slightly uncomfortable: was Stephen going to try to persuade me that the killer of the Dalzells had been suffering from diabolic possession? That he had tried to exorcise the demon and had failed?) I felt this was going a bit too far, and said so.

"I did suspect that Jane was seeing Meg again," Stephen replied. "But you must understand that she was very much in two minds about the whole thing. On the one hand, Meg and her mother had brought her up to fight capitalism, to be in a state of perpetual war with the society they lived in, and she was a radical by temperament, and on the other she wanted peace and harmony, which it seems she could never find. As for the diabolic qualities of Meg, I don't know how else you would describe them. Have you never felt real evil?"

"Well, what were these powers," I said again. No doubt Stephen wanted to protect his friend, whether she

37

was dead or alive, and by believing she had been 'possessed' at the time of the crimes he could condone them.

"I began to grasp them when I went to see Meg shortly after the murder of Mr Dalzell," Stephen said after a short pause. "Jane had recently seemed very agitated and confused and all the newspaper reports of his Scottish background, etc. made me uneasy. I knew she had seen Meg again and I wanted to try to have it out with her. But—and whether you believe this or not is up to you— Meg threw me off course from the beginning. I rang the bell and one of the small (female—the boys were sent away) children let me in. It was quite dark in the hall and there were rows of bicycles stacked there. Then the door of the red room, the visitors' room, opened. I saw Jane quite clearly standing against the light. One of the bicycles was in the way and I couldn't see her legs and feet, but from the waist up it was definitely Jane. The only snag was that I knew Jane was at a film showing the other side of London. I'd spoken to her just as she set off, so as to make sure I *wouldn't* bump into her when I went to see Meg. Then she turned and went back into the room, and Meg's voice called to me to come in. I went—and there was Meg and no-one else. I remember it was a very windy day, and cold, but the window was open at the top and some white blossom was blowing in. It had settled on Meg's hair, like confetti. But I can't think of a less likely bride! Well it's possible she was up to that kind of trick at Michael Dalzell's house and Jane wasn't there at all. It all depends on what you believe."

"It certainly does," I said. I knew I sounded cold, but

I was beginning to feel that Stephen wouldn't be the ideal witness, as I had hoped.

"So what did Meg say?" I went on.

"It was terrible. I realised that she had spun a web round Jane from which she would never be able to extricate herself. There was nothing, no method of persuasion she hadn't used. She'd persuaded Jane, I think, that if she killed her father and her half-sister, the Dalzell money would go to her, as the natural child—and if there was any trouble she, Meg, would see to it that there'd be a big court case, and all the women out in force. (All this I worked out afterwards, wondering about Meg's motives, but once I saw it was the money that was wanted for the group, it was simple.) I don't know how she convinced Jane she wouldn't be found out but, after all, none of them ever were. It was only since the second killing that I began to realise all this and then they'd all disappeared. It was an extraordinary gamble, for Jane coming forward and claiming the fortune would certainly have made her a suspect. But there was no proper evidence against her for either crime. The butler in Hampstead saw either two women, or one woman, and was so upset by the disguise, or change, or whatever it was, that he refused to swear to anything. In the case of the second killing, the girl was found in a street bleeding to death from a neck wound, at the time when there were plenty of witnesses who saw Jane at a party. They would have pulled it off if the vital ingredient hadn't vanished into thin air.

"Meg's method was to trap her victim in a dialectic of

madness. I'd never dreamed fanaticism could be carried to such lengths, and sound so purely and coolly lucid and convincing—once you'd been brainwashed, that is. I asked her if Mr Dalzell was in fact Jane's father because I worried about her, and about possible repercussions. 'I don't believe for an instant that Jane knows or cares,' Meg said. 'This is a paternalistic society. Mr Dalzell was a symbol of the father of all women.' 'A symbol?' I said. 'How can you see him as that? He's now a body in a morgue. Doesn't that make any difference to you?' 'His assassination was symbolic,' Meg replied. 'It was a ritual killing. The left hand performs the act figuratively, the right hand performs it literally. There is no difference between the two. He was the incarnation of capitalism. We have incarnated our disapproval of him.'

"I just didn't know what to say to all this. It's the modern evil, I believe, this jumble of Marxism and Tantrism and anything else thrown in, which is used to persuade people to kill each other. Meg went on to tell me that women had been defiled and degraded always, and particularly since the seventeenth century when they had been execrated as witches or elevated to virtuous wives. She said something about 'taking one of each' and I should have realised Dalzell's daughter was in danger but I didn't, for once again Meg confused me, and I thought she was still talking about the 'two-women-in-one' which she claimed was the root of the wrongs of society—the suppression of masculinity in women and of femininity in men. Had I thought then, too, that it was the money they wanted, I'd have been quicker."

"So Meg told you nothing definite." I was determined to get some facts, if I possibly could, but it was becoming clear to me that there was something quite unusual in the case. I knew I would have to hear more of this woman's crazy theories—the future, I fear, is on the way to becoming more and more like this, an endless display of a phenomenon I read somewhere described as 'evaginative pyrotechnics'. However, if only Stephen could remember Meg admitting to—or perhaps boasting—of the murders we could inform the police and mount a full scale search.

"No, no, she didn't say anything definite," Stephen said. "She said the power of the word would return through women, that it was when belief in the prophecies of witches and sybils ended that the word began to die."

"Oh yes," I said. I glanced quickly at Stephen. He sounded quite unmoved by Meg's wild ideas—I suppose he had heard them many times before. I flipped open the file and turned to the photographs of the body of the daughter of Michael Dalzell. They were a horrible sight. She was lying partly under a sheet but you could see her neck was badly torn. Her eyes, unlike her father's, were closed. She had what looked like a small tiara in her fair hair. "So you saw Jane before this—you've seen these, I presume?—happened?" I handed the police photographs over the desk. Stephen flinched and looked away from them. It crossed my mind that he had persuaded himself by now, to such a degree, of some kind of magical agency at work that he had forgotten the brute facts.

"Oh yes." Stephen put a hand over his eyes, then removed it again quickly. "I saw her that night. She wasn't well, but she wanted to go to the party. We'd been going to some strange parties then, I remember, mostly through Jane's boyfriend who was in the film world. We went to a party given by some rich people called Berring . . . and then, a few nights later . . . on the night . . ."

"And you honestly think she was responsible for the death of Michael Dalzell's daughter?"

"I don't know if that's who she thought it was, by then," Stephen said. He looked suddenly sad and tired. "Or if you could call her responsible. She seemed to be living in a perpetual state of sanctioned irresponsibility— the state induced by Meg, of course. And she couldn't have done it anyway, could she? She was seen at the party at the time the girl was killed."

"Unless it wasn't really her who was seen," I heard myself saying. I stopped short, and avoided meeting Stephen's eyes. "No . . . well," I corrected myself. "It was one of the gang perhaps—the point being that Jane lured her from the party to her death?"

"I just don't know." Stephen glanced in the direction of the document, which was lying on my desk, and said: "If I'd read that then, I would have done everything in my power to find her after that evening. Not that I would necessarily have succeeded. She was secretive about her movements. She never talked about her childhood. I wouldn't have known where to look."

"No." I stared down at the identikit pictures, all ridiculously dissimilar to each other, of the girl seen by passersby in Hampstead, and the girl seen in the street where Dalzell's daughter was found. There were photographs of

42

Jane in existence, of course, but it was hard to gauge anything about her from them. Her hair was blonde, but it looked as if it was probably tinted. Her face was curiously blank.

"What was Jane really like?" I said.

Stephen looked up at me, surprised. "I couldn't describe her. At her best she was confident, but too often she was very uneasy with herself. I was fond of her. Being with her made me feel interested in things. Yet she often said she wished she was someone else."

"Did she? This is a difficult era for women, I suppose."

"Oh yes. She was always searching for some 'missing male principle' or something."

"Poor Jane!"

For a time Stephen and I sat in silence, thinking of the sad and messy lives of Jane and women like her. Then Stephen said: "I think Meg's cleverness was in realising she couldn't gain her ends by crude political argument. Jane had been away from her world too long."

Again I hoped to steer the conversation away from this unprofitable area. I said:

"Would Jane inherit the Dalzell fortune if she were alive and came forward to claim it?"

"That I don't know." Stephen rose. I saw that his patience had come to an end. "Don't they wait seven years before you're declared officially dead? Then it'll go to a cousin, I suppose."

I had the feeling Stephen was a little annoyed that I hadn't taken his descriptions of Meg more seriously. He made his way to the door, and I made a point of showing him out of the house and thanking him warmly. I promised I would read Jane's journal and would let him know my impressions. On the doorstep he paused. "Meg was a kind of embezzlement," he said. I was surprised at his use of the word, and couldn't repress a smile. "An enravishment," he went on. "You must bear that in mind."

Then he went down the street. Because he was plump he had rather a waddling walk. I glanced at the address on the piece of paper he had handed me, and wondered if I would ever see him again. Then he turned the corner and was gone. Somehow I knew he hadn't told me where he really lived. And when I looked for him it turned out I was right. The address I'd been given, at the end of a wide street in Battersea, was that of an abandoned and boarded-up church.

I now present the strange 'journal' of the girl Jane. The poem printed overleaf was found among the pages of the journal, and I presume must have been copied out by her: what it signified to her I don't know. I will make no comment on the pages which follow, except to say there can seldom have been so forceful an example of the effect a fanatical mind can have on an impressionable one.

Edinburgh, July 1986

THE JOURNAL OF JANE WILD

Insomnia

by Marina Tsvetayeva

In my enormous city it is   night
as from my sleeping house I go   out
and people think perhaps I'm a daughter or wife
but in my mind is one thought only   night.

The July wind now sweeps a way for   me,
From somewhere, some window, music though   faint.
The wind can blow until the dawn   today,
in through the fine walls of the breast rib-cage.

Black poplars, windows, filled with   light.
Music from high buildings, in my hand a flower.
Look at my steps   following   nobody
Look at my shadow, nothing's here of me.

The lights   are like threads of golden beads
in my mouth is the taste of the night   leaf.
Liberate me from the bonds of   day,
my friends, understand: I'm nothing but your dream.

I'LL HAVE TO tell you now of the night I first went on my travels . . . the night, most of all, that Meg gave me further signs of her power.

I left the Berrings' party and walked home through the streets where it looked as if it had never rained, I walked fast in front of the dust gardens and the brick walls to keep people in, I sent cats up trees to perch heavy as fruit in the foggy grey leaves. As I walked on I could feel myself falling apart. I was in a frenzy of impatience to become another person. My rump was soft and divided under my clinging silk dress as men photographers would have it divide: ripe, ready for a mouthful to be taken out. My legs were thin and perched in high-heeled sandals, the pale tights making them all the more ridiculous and vulnerable. My breasts, unshielded, nosed the air for potential attackers like glow-worms swimming always a few inches in front of me. And yet—somehow—I got home! The streets had been very silent; tonight the menace hadn't come out in a humped back in grey gaberdine, or a gaggle of youths flying low like crows; it had lurked there, the urban forest, waiting for something impossible to come about.

I let myself into the house-converted-into-flats where I live and think every year will be the last. Look at the lino! That purple and cream scum whirling and foul smelling on the floor, dead blood and feathers. And the walls! Who made this elephantine pattern of chandeliers on a mango background, what grandeur did they think they were instilling there? As always, it is chilly in the hall and on the stairs. The overhead light, resplendent though it is, goes out after a minute with a popping sound from an odious black plastic button by my door. I am never at my door on time. I have to fondle this excrescence, caress it into being, so it will click on again and let me in through total darkness to my flat.

There are all the signs in the flat of Tony and I having gone out to the party in a bad mood. Once up the three stairs carpeted in hard cord, lights on and standing on the landing, I can smell us there together: from the sitting room, where we drank cold Stolichneya vodka before we left and Tony complained at me spending too much of my money on it; in the bedroom, which is just on my left, I can see the dresses and skirts I tried on and then threw on the bed in despair. The whole place feels both over-occupied and totally empty. Perhaps I never will return.

I can imagine how Tony is doing at the party. He has a small affected smile on his face and he is pretending he isn't working his way ever nearer to the daughter of an American film producer who might make his life a little more exciting for him. Although he's a screenwriter, the editor of a literary quarterly has just asked him to write on the new Spanish cinema. Tony is secretly more pleased by this than by an offer to write a Hollywood blockbuster. He can't forget Cambridge, and the poets and writers in old tweed jackets who give a short surprised laugh when they bump into Tony now. Or perhaps he has been trapped by Fay Langham. She is telling him about feminist cinema. His eyes are wandering, his tongue suddenly becomes dry. "Let me get you a drink, Fay." I laugh as I go into the bedroom and then into the tiny bathroom beyond.

There was no time to lose. The familiarity of the flat had deflected me for a moment, and had reconciled me to my skin—I sat in both uneasily for so many years that it was hard to imagine I could change. But now it was happening. I sat down on the bed because the floor seemed to be moving under me. Over the pile of discarded clothes, the scarlet flowers on black background, black roses on white nylon crêpe de chine, layered skirts and flimsy tops, I reached for the scissors that lay on the table beside my bed. I picked them up and my hand brushed the soft dresses: I thought of Meg—Meg whom I had seen again tonight, her dress of gypsy handkerchiefs and the eyes that had made me turn on my heel and leave the party as if I had immediately read her command. I hadn't expected her to follow me. But I knew that she knew tonight was my first real chance to escape.

With the scissors I started to hack at my hair. Long pieces of blonde hair, high-lighted every three months and slightly curled for the party, fell onto the rumpled clothes. I almost immediately felt calmer and more peaceful. I wandered to the bathroom, and watched my

49

face look out as naked and surprised as a sheep at shearing. Aren't you trying to cut it properly? my eyes seemed to be saying back to me from the mirror. This is a terrible thing to do. *Think* how long it'll take to grow out again!

I shrugged at the reflection and strolled this time to the bedroom window, still hacking away with the scissors, which seemed to have taken on a determination of their own despite the protests of the owner of the hair. I pulled back the curtains, leaned on the window sill and looked out. I had often imagined myself flying on my broomstick from here—as my mother flew on that icy night after the brawl—but she fell, even the strength of her beliefs couldn't keep her in the air, and when they took her from the bank of snow to the lorry she knew the battle was lost. I would fly so as not to be with Tony any more, so as not to be me. Yet Tony could go if we decided it wasn't working out. We didn't have to marry. I didn't even have the risk of pregnancy: an I.U.D. like a computer gadget lay inside me, with a thin cord for removal if I decided to 'start a family'. How many times had I dreamed of launching myself from that window sill, floating into the black night until I banged up against the stars! And now I was going, but by a different route, and into quite another Universe.

The scissors had reached my fringe and decimated it, little spikes of straw stood on my head and it was quite rough when I ran my hands through it, like stroking a pig's back. For the first time since childhood I could see by looking straight ahead, instead of shaking my fringe to one side, a gesture which, over the years, had become apologetic and feminine, as if I had to admit it wasn't my right to contemplate the world. I laid the scissors on the sill and looked down into the street—for the last time, I thought. A sort of rage came over me, and the night air, with an abrupt coldness, gave me the sensation my body had shrunk.

Down on the right, near the junction with the High Street, is the house run by the kind woman with big brown eyes, the house for the battered women of the neighbourhood and their children; but the most successful lesbian nightclub in London, Paradise Island, is next door to them, and the men who pass smile and shift uncomfortably at the mixture of misfits: the women who had the foolishness not to stop themselves from being beaten up, the great lakes of blue bruise on their faces and arms an unacceptable disfigurement, and the women who want each other, whose breasts meet like soft pillows as they dance. In the mornings the bottles come out on the pavement in front of Paradise Island. They look desolate: empty tonic, empty bitter lemon, hundreds of empty litre bottles of wine. Somewhere, scattered in their different flats, the women are sleeping it off. But when it's hot in that street, and the old man further down away from the High Street puts his parrot out on the door-step, and the parrot calls out with a sound so alien that you feel there is no chance, ever, of one human being understanding another, and the smart young Persians opposite turn up their record players in their sunflower-papered rooms, then it's time to wonder what happened, to shut the window before you fall, and make, as far as possible, a construction of a day.

Now I did close the window, for some of my fear was still with me. I went back to the bathroom and re-examined my appearance. Women and mirrors; mirrors and women. My face seemed to have grown much smaller and my eyes were round and rimmed with exhaustion, black as the underside of a moth. My hair stood in tufts all over my head. I would have smiled but my mouth, which looked thinner, was clamped together. I wondered if my teeth were different underneath.

I could see the foot of the bed in the mirror. My heart missed a beat: a pair of legs in blue jeans was lying there! Then I saw that it was blue jeans alone. And a straight jacket, also made of denim. I went towards them. I looked down at my body before I pulled off the silk party dress. My breasts were tiny now, and the bra that had once contained them looked large and empty. Like a shroud, I thought, as I stood there paralysed a moment, unable to move. Although it was ordinary modern gear that lay there on the bed, to pull on these trousers from an unknown world was like stepping into death.

The first thing that happened as I changed my clothes was a complete reconstruction of the party I had just been to with Tony—it flashed before my eyes, colours muted, but with cast complete. First I saw the people I liked there: Gala, Stephen. Then I saw Tony, being patronising with a literary agent, frowning down into his glass as if an important truth was to be found at the bottom, like those mugs with a frog. I saw the hostess, rich, American: her walls hung with brown silk, shit silk money. Her hair was rich brown curls; her head was tilted back; she liked mixing people. There was a man who ran a famous gambling club talking to an ex-socialist historian. A Chinese-American hooker who said she had just come from Brando. Then I saw Meg. Meg's eyes were fixed on me. I felt the floor moving under my feet and the hostess's splendid pink candelabra went dim.

By this time I was ready. I was narrow-hipped, not too tall. There was a gun in the pocket of the denim jacket. I went out of the flat, shoved the black plastic button, and was over the petrified lino steps three at a time.

I am out in the street, I think I can see Tony coming towards me, a little drunk from the party, weaving slightly as he walks. Yes—we passed—three feet apart. He didn't even give me a glance.

WHERE WAS I going? My new body seemed to know.
I was walking fast, but smooth and controlled, and I was
heading for the High Street. The street where I lived
looked already like a ruin excavated a hundred years ago:
as if the houses had been built with their deformities,
crazed pipes, broken roofings, ghastly follies in the worst
of Victorian taste. The light from the slit-eyed lamps was
lunar. Women stared at me as they went into Paradise
Island. They hesitated at the sight of me: I was unplace-
able perhaps, a new genetic pattern like a neon sign in
cuneiform, something ancient and known and at the same
time infinitely strange. I didn't smile at them, so they
remained unsmiling back. Their lips were hard, the
colour of prunes.

And I passed the house of the battered women. There
was one light on at the top of the house. It was a bedside
lamp, with a pale blue frilly shade. This pale blue light
showed up two heads, and two bodies in black jumpers
and skirts. The room behind them was dark as a cave.
They sat immobile there, in this distant, parodic memory
of the primeval beach—the blue light thin as water
around their scarcely breathing forms, the cave an illu-

sion, four walls in reality, property of the Council, dark, stretching back to the days of their birth and the first astonished burst into the sunshine of the untouched beach, four walls of crumbling lath and plaster, a temporary refuge, a mock womb before it was time to move on again. One of the women was knitting. She looked down on me with less concern than the women who had gone into Paradise Island. Her options were closed. She had copulated with the wrong man. She had been sterilised now, as a punishment for her mistakes, and she sat quietly, drawn to the artificial light below, its stern lack of mystery resembling hers. Her eyes were empty and black, like a moonless sky. And, to reassure myself, I looked up beyond her at the moon. It was there tonight, whether people would have it or not: wisps of black cloud danced over its face. Whether man had climbed on it or not, it still smiled sardonically. And I smiled— thinking of the facial twitch, the smirk, which would send them off into unending space, like swatted flies.

I was at the end of the street, by the corner super- market, the compound for the women who are neither battered nor dyke. The channels are narrow, and iron gates, like automated warders, bang against the knees. The women smile at the cheerful goods. Who knows but one day, unwrapping the bright tartan package, mile on mile of paper, some crinkled as corrugated iron, some transparent and horribly soft, membrane, caul, out will fall the wax doll with the pin in its heart, the scapegoat for all this. Then it will have been worth it! Until then, the Pandora's boxes hold vertigo and fear, and fear of closed spaces and fear of open spaces and a drowsiness while operating machinery. In the dark corners of the boxes, the still unwrapped portions, under the Free Gift Offer, lies the forgotten past. The women pull and tear at the little white worms of paper that make the wadding. Then the box lies open and shallow. It has revealed nothing at all.

Tonight there are only representations of these women in the supermarket, for the supermarket is closed. Cardboard women, shown to be beautiful for their sojourn there, and in their cardboard surrounds, at least, bathed in colour. Some of them hold boxes of objects to eat, others boxes of objects which will absorb their blood, some hold a pink drink. I bow to them as I pass. Hi! I feel sympathy for them: they can reign at night, when their alter egos aren't bustling and shopping in the compound, but unlike me they are locked in with the darkened goods. They can contemplate the shelves. They love the boxes, they gaze at them in total self-absorption.

The High Street is wider than I remembered. There is no traffic. The islands look as if they would sink if boarded; glacial mannequins wave from distant shops; in all this, which is like a muted cruise, a secret departure at night for Purgatory, I am walking several feet above the ground and with my hand firmly on the pistol in the pocket of my coat. This time others are at risk, not me. I am looking for someone to kill. And as I pass the fluorescent reds and yellows, the prayers and exhortations to eat and sleep and breathe for the sake of the manufacturers alone, I exult in my new power. I might fire a bullet at the perplexed, wrinkled brow of Burt Lancaster as he struggles on the poster level with my head. I might blacken the teeth of the housewife suspended in the vapours of her pie, her smile moistened in the wreaths of animal fat coming up at her like winter breath. Or I might shoot at the steeple of the church, which is encircled by motorway now: if the elastic were pulled any tighter it would snap and fall. But I'll save my fire. I may need it later on.

There is a strong smell of the sea at the end of the street. Dead, flat sea trapped in walls, sea heavy with driftwood and speckled with the white bellies of dead fish, a scum of sawdust by the gangways to the ships. I can see the masts standing in the port. The smell quickens my step. I am bringing the smell with me. The moon rests at a cock-eyed angle to the highest mast, string slipping, clouds bob over like streamers and are gone into the night. I arrive at the port. So this is where I will disembark for another world! On one of these great liners, filled with orange light and soundless activity. Dancing on the deck, sailing into warm, opaque waters so deep they seem to balance the sky above them like a plate. Going up in a cloud of spray to pierce the ether. But first, I must find my prey.

The first thing I see is that I am in the centre of the port. Its wide arms embrace the ships, the strips of pavement and the shadowy cafés with lights and onion-braids of sponges hanging by the doors and blue round sailors' hats thrown down. There is no movement in the water at all. Not even the smallest boat nudges the jetty. I can see people walking about inside the big liners—it looks as if they're making ready to cast off any minute—and more people in the cafés. But not a sound. Are they all dead already? Have I come too late? I pull the gun from my pocket and make my way along the right hand tentacle of the harbour. I will go into the first bar. I will accomplish my mission, as they say in Men Talk on TV. And then I will be free to go.

The bar is stained with green light when I go in. Bars of green on the sailors' faces, like shutters hiding their eyes and distorting the curve of their jaws. Pools of green on the surface of the bar where there are half-drained glasses and plates of crumbling, soft nuts. I cock the gun and point it at the room. Green smoke comes down steadily from the roof, as if expelled from the mouth of an amateur theatrical dragon. It blows into my eyes. I fire the gun at the first sailor in my range, who is sitting with his chin cupped in his hands at the nearest table. He slumps to the ground. But the shot was noiseless, and so was his death. It's not what I had hoped.

Now the sailor is dead all the others crowd round and beg me not to kill them. They clasp at my waist, and we dance without sound. When I drink, the green liquid scorches my throat, and when I see myself in the glass, through the verdigris and the smudged filth from the sailors' hands, I see why they want me so. In my perfect androgyny, my face round as a mermaid's, my mouth black and slit like a wound from a knife, my legs like a young stevedore's—with the rime of green under my fingernails that tells how long I have been under the sea, hair growing upward, sucked by the bubbles, waving like weed in the cold green current—like a treasure long lost at sea, embedded in nacreous green rock, shifted here and there on the sandy floor by shoals of spotted fish, I am for them the dread of their seafaring days: the siren with a cracked voice who lures them to the bottom of the sea, the forgotten woman and half-man who make up the Angel of Death. In the deep, sub-aqueous silence we dance on, for I know now they will never let me go. In sea years, they are a long time dead.

In the port, the biggest liner pulls out. No sound, just the orange lights in the cabins—and I can see a Latin American band, all orange satin frills and soundless maracas on the forward deck. A steward ushers guests aft, to wave us all goodbye. Champagne corks are forced from bottles, silently they fly up to the sky. Everyone waves. I am whirled faster and faster round.

My hand lay curled on the floor by the bed. Blood had gone down into the fingers, and they were bunchy and red: they felt as if they had been trussed by the butcher and then cut apart again. The palm looked up at the ceiling, mottled, the lines of destiny like faint pencil marks on the flesh. On one line, which marched across the hand and disappeared over the other side in a delta of fainter etchings, a strong, adventurous exploration of the upper side, the side it never could see without taking the inexorable step, I had walked for a while last night. But I had, literally, missed the boat. I was to be kept here a while yet, on the inner track.

Tony's back faced me on my left. I pulled up my hand

from the floor, and before the blood crept down my
fingers I felt it for a moment make an independent movement, in the direction of the door, as if the invisible body
to which it was attached had decided to go out. No such
luck for me! I was still only half in myself and I must lie
still until things were right again or I might vanish
altogether. I must contemplate Tony's back. Shoulder
blades, freckles. Matrons, soap, thin shoulder blades in
sports blazers, white aertex shirts open-pored over
freckles, like tiny molluscs living on the skin that must be
allowed to breathe. Thick white clouds over too many
dark rhododendrons. Tony's beautiful feet in white
plimsolls, which hardly seem to anchor him to the ground
as he runs over the grass. I think of Tony like that
because that's where he's stuck: twenty years later still
the prep school boy: charming, eager to get on but
tentative; would the effort of becoming a man break him
up and turn him to dust? No, he need never change.

Bells were ringing in the church at the end of the street.
I had forgotten it was Sunday—a day to pray for good, to
pray for strength to fight the evil world into which I
would soon be abducted. But a pleasant laziness came
over me at the thought. Who said that where I was going
was evil? Why make out that the present world had
anything good to say for itself? In this godless street only
the old man with the parrot went to church, leaving the
parrot haughty and outraged in the window of his front
room. And some of the old women, shoe-horned from
attic rooms at the sound of the bells, their heads grey as
winter cabbages, flesh in bulges all down their bodies

under their coats. Did they pray to go into the next world just as they were now? Or did they think it would be something quite extraordinary, a real shock, but well worth getting down on stiff knees square with pain to ask for, one eye on the vicar's pointed black shoe under his skirt.

Tony moved, and the shoulder blades went down under him as he turned on his back. No matter: I was myself again now, I could deal with his sleeping profile. Ageless in sleep, I saw that he belonged to another century, a time when the important thing for a man was to go away and then to return again, a long crusade, a dusty journey home in a column of armoured men glinting like fish scales under the foreign sun. Once home, he could enjoy his tomb, and the placid skies of Southern England beyond the crypt. But now, poor Tony, with his script conferences in Rome and Zurich and the rubber corridors of the airport: he was always setting off and returning, to no avail.

Tony's eyes opened. It was a melancholy sight, for as the lids lifted I felt his uncertainty, and his depression with the world, and his puzzlement at the wall opposite, as if he had never been here in his life before. Then I felt annoyed. I had been a long way, further than him. I even despised his dreams. Yet his foolish frown at the wall, with its Victorian oil of a pig he had bought in the market a year ago and a Paris May '68 poster I had once put up (it was a dark bilious yellow, de Gaulle's power-saw nose had been ripped at the edge), suggested he had no real desire to be here at all. It was as if he had come for a one night stand and stayed two years, after a drugged potion, an uneasy sleep.

"Do you want coffee?"

I always address Tony as a guest, although we share the bills of the flat. In fact, he has made almost no impression on the flat, which is as hard and gloomy—in the ridiculous red brick building with the artificially grand hall, the syringa bush outside and the irritating unmown grass by the gate where cuckoo spit collects in summer and brushes my bare legs, and then is gone again—as before he arrived here. What difference *could* he have made? Sometimes I think, although Tony may imagine he's returning from these journeys to me, it's really his mother he yearns for. Ah, Mrs Marten! When will her next visitation be? Her thin legs, her jerking arms. The flat is mine in name only, she is the white magnet that draws him and me and the rooms we live in, she controls us and burns us dry. He leaps like a mouse to the sound of her voice. Yet, as if it's too unbearable to marry a son and mother in this way, I often think instead of his past life, in another flat, with another girlfriend. I imagine him transformed, radiant: the girl is pliable and dark. What do these words mean? That I want him to have been capable once, at least, of being the other side of himself? And is my vision of the girl just another escape from my own skin into the opposite? I suppose so. Tony and I—as we are—are not very convincing.

He noticed my hair. He asked me what the hell I'd done that for.

"I don't know. I just did it. Last night."

"Obviously. It wasn't like that at the Berrings."

"Why? Does it look so awful?"

"Of course it does."

"But men cut their hair off like that. Why shouldn't I?"

"Suit yourself."

I went into the bathroom. What was the point of going on like this? Certainly my face looked odd, but it was what I felt like at the moment rather than a picture to please someone else. I was in a transitional stage. The strawy spikes standing on my head announced my state of siege. I brushed my teeth and looked around for the jeans and denim jacket on the floor. There was no sign of them. My heart sank.

"I'm making scrambled eggs," Tony said from the bedroom.

I heard him walk past on his way to the kitchen and I stared at myself intensely in the mirror. Sometimes his movements in the flat were like the stealings-up of an enemy spy, sometimes an outright military takeover. I could never tell where he would be next. I dreaded meeting him in the passage, as if our passing there only underlined our meaningless lives in which we were anyway going in the opposite direction to each other.

"Do you want scrambled eggs or not?"

"Have you by any chance seen a pair of jeans anywhere?"

I had given myself away. If they weren't there I didn't know what I would do. I thought of the outside of the building where I lived, the pretentious façade that made it, the only block of flats in the street, the kind of building

63

where people scrawl insults in chalk on the lower walls. I saw myself going out, in jeans and jacket, walking on air, and coming back in the clinging silk dress. What had happened? Why had the other world rejected me like this?

"Yes. I put them in the washbox. I'm making the eggs now."

This brought me out of the bathroom. I had a bath towel round me, which emphasised my fatness and my sloping shoulders. I went along the passage to the kitchen, already a victim for Tony, unable to wait for what he had to say.

"Why . . . why did you put them in the washbox?"

"They're not yours, are they? They looked far too small. I thought you must have got into some tangle with someone." He looked at me oddly. "What the hell's going on, Jane? With your hair and everything?"

"But why were they dirty? They didn't have . . . blood on them, or anything?"

Tony forked the eggs out onto plates. He set his marble profile above them and began to eat.

"No, they weren't dirty. They had a strange smell. Like burnt matches, rather."

I went back to my bedroom smiling. So the other world smelled of sulphur, did it? I would have to consult Meg on this. And I put on my 'normal' clothes with a light heart: a cotton skirt that had gone at the waist so that the zip had to be dragged up to the waistband and stuck there, a green T shirt and floppy white sandals. I wouldn't be needing them much longer, if my other outfit was really lying in the washbox; and they felt already like a dead woman's clothes, neither in nor out of fashion, slightly embarrassing and poignant. I pulled back my shoulders and walked at a quick march to the kitchen and the scrambled eggs. One of Tony's virtues, which went with his low expectations of life, was his lack of curiosity: he would almost certainly fail to ask me what I really *had* been up to the night before. He didn't like surprise, which he treated as if it were sudden pain, backing away from something unforeseen, however pleasurable, with a hurt, blinking stare. If—which he must have suspected— I had picked up a youth, played with lighted matches, fallen with him in waste ground somewhere beyond the refinement of our street and shopping precinct, Tony didn't want to know about it. And, sure enough, we had our coffee and eggs in silence while the brimstone-tainted jeans lay, carefully covered with the lid, in the straw box in the corner.

"There's a press showing today," I said at last. We either talked about the films I went to and wrote about, or the progress of Tony's script. Tony, with his gloomy standing invitation to bad luck, was involved in a script of Conrad's *Chance*, and had already announced that there was a jinx on Conrad in the film business, things never worked out as they should. Secretly I didn't blame Conrad for cursing people like Tony. Why couldn't they leave his work alone?

"It's a West German film," I said to Tony's half-questioning look. "About two men who wander the roads on a lorry."

"*Easy Rider*, German style," Tony said. "Why're they showing it on a Sunday?"

"The Schroeders always do. Don't you remember, you came to one."

"No lunch then?"

No lunch.

I got up, feeling vaguely guilty as always. Sunday lunch was supposed to be a cementing thing for couples: you could see the woman fingering bleeding meat on the Friday, frowning over the joints as if the secret of their future happiness lay in the grain of the flesh. Yorkshire pudding solidified relationships too, producing a drowsiness after the meal, a soft acceptance of everything. I would be sitting watching the screen instead of preparing all this. And Tony would be hard and distant as a result. All for a portion of an animal. But offerings were important. Without the smell of roasting meat from the beaches below, the gods might have turned away from the world.

"I'll do the meat," Tony said. "I'm only juggling around with the script this morning. Did I tell you, it looks as if Susannah York might be Flora de Barral."

"It's not true!"

"You think she'd be right for the part?"

I tried to give an encouraging smile, and failed. What on earth did it matter? I certainly wouldn't be going to a press showing of *that* one. And at the moment, because I knew I would be leaving soon, travelling to places where, in a million years of searching, Tony would never find me, I felt a great warmth towards him, an affection filled with regret that I would be losing him too. I went over to where he was sitting and put my arms round his head. I brought my chin down on the top of his head. There was no parting in the thick brown hair, which smelled of toast. How would he manage without me? Perfectly well, was the answer as I straightened up again. He would hardly notice I had gone!

"It's just that I don't want lunch today," I said. "I'm thinking of going to see Gala after the film."

"Oh."

"You don't mind, do you?"

"Of course not!"

"Very well then."

After this exchange, in which I apparently conveyed total heartlessness and from which Tony emerged downcast, I went with too buoyant a step to the door of the flat. He was watching me as I left, but there was no way to present my physical departure acceptably. If I walked like a woman cowed by thousands of years behind the veil, eyes down, erect, shuffling gait, there was no reason for me to be allowed out at all and I would be unable to get as far as the main door of the building. If I went 'ordinarily', as Tony would go, simply walking out of the flat with a quick wave, it would be selfish, uncaring. If I were coming back for the meat, of course, I could make a quick apologetic dash of my departure for my job. But I wasn't. So I went with an energy that was clearly provocative. Tony's sulky glowering face came out with me into the darkness of the stairs and hung in front of me like the after-image of a violently bright light as I groped my way towards the black plastic button. I heard his silence affect the whole building, and it hung over me like a hood until I was halfway down the street.

There is a wind blowing today, the air in the street is milky white, and scraps of white paper float along at first floor level. The street is as different today from the black stillness of the night before as I in my cotton skirt and plodding step, am changed from the creature who flew down it. Since then, the full bottles that went in to Paradise Island have been emptied and are set out on the pavement for collection. The supermarket, still closed because it's Sunday, reflects in its plate glass windows the ghostly figures of the women who will go in and become enclosed there tomorrow. A noise comes from the wives' shelter: children, pent up, and suffering from the misery of their mothers, pelted, like the street, with mysterious scraps of words, nervous in the hot wind which also blows white dust into the open windows and flaking paint of the surrounds. I walk up to Notting Hill Gate, where the press showing of the film is being held. The flowers in the sloping gardens are smothered with the fine white dust. One householder, rich and proud, has a sculpture six feet wide and twice as tall in his front garden—it looks like the head of a white tulip, two of the heavy stone petals peeled back to reveal the empty centre. In a poorer street, where the railings of the houses seem to press against them, allowing only a mantrap-size descent into the basement, someone has propped a flying figure in white papier mâché at the top of the steps: one leg and one arm are flung out into the street, the eyeless face, like the

68

face of a victim of an accident, swathed in white plaster bandages, gazes at the houses across the strip of grey concrete. I feel a sudden fear, as I walk past, that this is someone like me, someone who tried to escape, punished by the world, frozen into a ludicrous figure, not even made of hard substance but ready to melt into shreds of pulp at the first burst of rain. Or is it all that is left of the Snow Queen, this white, artificial, sexless thing, after her splinters of ice had gone out into the world and she had fallen from her cold throne? The rich smell of Sunday dinners cooking, the red meat spitting in this white bottomless world gives me nausea. I have to cling onto a railing, at the end of the street of the arrested, flying figure, before I go on up the hill.

I know or recognise most of the film critics standing outside the cinema. They have tired, blank eyes from seeing too much of other people's fantasies, and are annoyed too at having their Sunday morning taken away from them. One or two nod to me. "Yes, but did you see that other Fassbinder?" "He comes in at the end of this—the Wenders, you know." "I know. But I mean, did you see that very early one?" They seem to be mouthing the words, the door of the cinema is shut, and they are agitated and anxious, longing for the film to be over and for Sunday lunch. What is the film going to show us? Life in contemporary society, it says on the hand-out. The apathetic, passive, alienated life, an odyssey without any point of return. I would rather watch a pearl grow in an oyster! I stand amongst the velvet trousers in the small crowd, and wonder if Meg will really send me away from all this. She once said, cryptically, that she would show me everything, all that was inside me, and all the different regions that can be reached without taking a step. I believed her. I stand thinking of tomorrow, when we will meet. Already, last night's journey seems far away, like a flash from a distant meteor. "Jane!" One of the critics, a short man with a frown, comes towards me in the white air. "Tell me, what did you think of the Skolimowski? They showed it again the other night. And I wondered if you'd seen it when it first came out . . ."

"The best foreign film to be made in England." I hear myself offering this stupid remark, but I remember the film well. It is violent, obsessive, surprising: as if a whole layer of England had been peeled off, the whiteness scrubbed away, and the underside, people's real passions and feelings, pushed up into the light. The critic nods as if I had said something interesting, and we begin to file into the cinema.

It is as we pass into the first dusk of the foyer that I see the girl. I stand for a moment, clutching my press card, waiting for her to turn and see me. So Meg answers me when I think of her! She has sent me this girl. And yet . . .

The girl turns. What is it that is so familiar about her? She has something of mine. We have been bound in an ancient story, of bitterness and revenge. Yet I feel I have never seen her before in my life. I can see that she recognises me too, for her eyes flicker and the message from her skin is one of familiarity. A small triumphant smile compresses the corners of her mouth. What did she do to me? Or was I the victor and is she, at peace now while I suffer, regarding me with pity and contempt? I move slightly in her direction, with a stumbling movement as if my knees have forgotten how to function while I walk. She stiffens at this, and glides into the cinema, but her stiffness is an invitation. Her head is full of pictures for me. I follow her into the dark red darkness, and sit down behind her, in the second row.

The film begins. In black and white, it says on the screen. But it's not the real blackness, nor the real whiteness: it's grey. A grey motorway stretches out on the screen above our heads. As it soars upwards, making us, the audience, like tiny creatures at the side of the road, my eyelids bisect it and come down halfway over my eyes —and through my lashes, which are trembling slightly with the effort of staying in that position, the first flickering blobs of colour begin to appear.

My mother was in the kitchen. The kitchen door led straight out onto the hill: there was no yard, just the grass that was always wet, either with rain or heavy dew: it went up in furrows to the line of Douglas firs planted as a windbreak by the grandfather of the laird; it was humped, long bolsters of grass which seemed to move on the steep hill when the rain swept into the valley from the west. On the grass were small white mushrooms, ex-humed every morning from the deep, stony land, and sheep, fleece yellowing with rain and faces oddly patterned as if with their markings they could signal something to each other. Beyond the line of firs and the half-broken stone wall grew the scratchy heather. I went up the cleuch sometimes, to search for cloudberries, those strange fruit which look like a drawing in a medical student's textbook, of internal organs stitched together: their taste is acrid and they grow only above the cloud line, tinges of red on their pink fleshy surface suggesting a faint scorch from the few moments when the clouds part and the sun comes down on them. But my mother used to like to make cloudberry jelly. I took a basket and I would pick blae-berries too, but sometimes the laird and his party were on the hill above our cottage, shooting from the holes in the ground burrowed out for them, or collecting the dusty purple blaeberries, and then I would have to slide back down the hill over bumps of heather and harebells to the grass and the kitchen back door.

What had my mother done? When the laird poked his head round the back—he always tried the front door first, forgetting that cottagers keep their front doors locked and the front rooms like small mausoleums behind them—she would go crimson, as if he had caught her stealing some of his property while he looked on. He had given her the cottage. He often referred to this as I stood at the door between the kitchen and the escape to the hill behind. She always thanked him, but went on looking guilty. Why was she so uneasy, fingering the old black skirt she wore, gazing past me at the hill as if she was longing to run for it and disappear into the white mist that came down the cleuch at midday every day and stayed there until rain and dark cloud brought on night. She had been his mistress, of course: some part of me understood that even when I was very young. I was his daughter.

That was why she was allowed to live in the cottage. The way he looked at me was furtive and eager, like the stare of a man searching for evidence of disease on his own body. He never touched me if he could help it. Yet he and my mother often looked vaguely at me and through me at the same time, as parents do when discussing ordinary matters in front of their children. Sometimes I felt I belonged to both of them, and then the cottage and the kitchen seemed to grow—and I did too, suddenly seeing into some bright space where there would be infinite possibilities. Soon, though, my mother would catch herself out in this relaxed attitude, and so would he — and Meg would be seen, walking up from the Burn Wood in her long skirts—and they would return to a combination of embarrassment and resentment, and the gloom, the stone floors, the stone sided sink, the thin wooden table with the gay plastic cloth seemed more oppressive than before. When there was sun, it was all right to go out the back: the light blue sky over the hills looked as if it could be reached in a minute, peewits and larks were everywhere, the gurgle of burn sounded loud as it slipped down out of sight to a hidden loch. But there was so seldom sun. The valley was steep. It looked, on a black day, as if its contours had been drawn with slashing lines on rough paper, and as if the lines contained our sentence, my mother's and mine. For our sins, we should stay here forever. And as it was clear she had practically no money, there seemed no way of getting out at all.

I'd seen the girl several times, the laird's real daughter. I'd been up the narrow mud road that led to our exile's cottage, and stared down at the large white house where she lived with her father and mother. She had a thin, bony, Scottish face, with grey eyes and fair hair, and always a slight smile of self-satisfaction at the corners of her mouth; she bounced an old red rubber ball against the wall of the kitchen garden as I watched her from the moorland above; sometimes her hair was tied in bunches and I knew it went a little frizzy in the rain. I was completely and obsessively jealous of her. I was her shadow, and she mine. By the time we went to the village school together, for we were almost exactly the same age, I think we both knew we were sisters. We fought in the school playground, which was a small stretch of concrete slung high in the hills, on the outskirts of the laird's small village. I went up on the seesaw, which was made from the thick trunk of a felled tree, and she went down; she went up, her eyes excited, grey as the drizzle that fell continually on us, her hooked, bony nose and thin mouth hovering over me, while I was down on the ground. One day she got up and walked away when I was up in the air, and I came crashing down. The teacher looked the other way.

My mother called to me from the kitchen to come in. It was the summer holidays: long, empty, grey days. Today the jeep would come along the mud track, over the top of the hill, and the laird and his party would spread rugs out in front of our cottage, on the sloping grass by the overflowing burn. In the gentle rain, watched by sheep, they would eat pies and hardboiled eggs and drink beer and wine, leaving the cans and bottles for my mother to collect. Then, flushed, they would go slowly up the hill to their holes. I was never allowed to be there. But if the daughter was with them she would twist on her rug and gaze at the windows of the house. Her mother, fair-haired as her daughter, and self-contained, also with an expression of secret amusement on her face most of the time, never turned to look at the cottage. When she walked back to the jeep with the picnic basket after lunch, it was always head down, eyes on the thin grass by the track, and the sheep droppings, and the ugly colt's foot that grew there, yellow and darkened with rain.

"Can't you see it's raining?"

Of course; it was always raining. My mother was using it as a pretext to get me in from the grass in front of the cottage. She came halfway towards me from the back of the house. Her head was jerking in the direction of the track; she must have heard the jeep. I saw she was crying. My mother's eyes were blue. When she cried they were like the water of the burn, bursting its banks. I went stiff, with anger at the life we led here. I stood my ground.

"You'll be soaked. Anyway, they're coming. Jane! Hurry up!"

My mother scurried up the bank and disappeared round the back of the house. In the past she would have dragged me with her—perhaps a part of her now, exhausted by the repressions of the past years, wanted a showdown of some kind. Indecision as to whether to move or not kept me rooted to the spot. And the jeep reared up on the crest of the hill. The engine was roaring, in first gear, the wheels were coated with mud.

"Jane!" My mother tried calling me one more time, from behind the window of the front room, and her voice sounded distant and resigned. I turned to face the jeep. Rain ran down the windows and the faces of the other mother and daughter were distorted, like the sound of my own mother's voice. Ishbel, for that was the name of my sister, looked as if she had been painted grotesquely onto the window, in thick white paint, and yellow for the streaks of her hair down her face. I made no movement, but watched them park the jeep, and push the doors open, and from the back two Labradors sprang out so there was an instant movement of sheep on the side of the hill.

On the screen in front of me the men are wandering the roads with their lorry. They are passive, looking for meaning, resigned to the fact they will find no more than the half-buried roots of their own childhood. They are lonely, but have blocked off their hunger and loneliness behind expressionless faces and obsession with technology and film. They can't live with women, but they can't live without them, for their wandering seems so absurd, so unlike any real journey of exploration of the past.

The girl in the row in front of me—Ishbel—looks at this sad whining end of the age of the conquistadors in silence. When the audience laughs she remains silent. The music is sad and persistent, not unlike bagpipe music I used to hear coming from inside the white walls of her house when her/our father gave a party. I sit tensely behind her. She had what I wanted. She had what should have belonged to me. What is she doing here now, what

of mine has she got her hands on now? She is an omen.
And there above our heads, on the grey flat roads of the
over-discovered world, the men neither of us want go
aimlessly about their lives. What shadow battle will she
and I fight next?

I knew what I was going to do. I leapt the burn while the
pale stockinged legs of the laird and his party were still
coming out of the jeep, and I ran up through wet bracken
to the wretched line of trees by the wall at the top of the
hill. These firs, straight and black, with wispy branches at
the top hardly strong enough to support a wood pigeon,
had no doubt been planted to protect the shepherd and
his sheep from the terrible winds, the snow drifts that
came at the speed of wind, the rain that was like having a
bucket emptied in your face. But they were our bars. They
surrounded our small prison, our patch of sheep-nibbled
grass—in the long Northern evenings, when the sky went
dim behind them and I was sitting out on the collection of
rough pebbles that made up our front garden I would
reach my arms out to them sometimes, prise them apart
and squeeze them together again. Wherever you looked,
there they were, except for the cleuch, of course, and what
was the point of thinking you could escape up that boggy
face that led to nowhere? Stumbling to the invisible
horizon, clamped under mist, walking on dead legs
deeper and deeper into the peat. It was fifteen miles to the
next crofter's cottage, and much further to the town.

I would hack my way out, and take my mother with me.
I stood thin behind the tallest tree on the hill. My hands

clasped the wet bark. It was scaly, unpleasant, like some
sea animal which has struggled to shore and grown a thin
fuzz of fur. The soft, wet wood dug in under my fingernails. I thought of the school, and Ishbel walking along
the road to the school. She always looked confident and
happy. My mother never used that road—the few times
she left the laird's land to go shopping in the small store
beneath the school she walked along the side of the hill on
a sheep track. They were treating her like a sheep. I was
some animal they would never even look at, although the
law insisted I should go to school. I looked down at the
jeep, and saw Ishbel climb out, stand exposed on the
grass, yet blurred by the constant rain.

Suddenly I felt something watching me. I turned round:
the track, planted on either side with a bristle of young
firs stretched in a straight line across a wash of grass and
heather to the white house, down in the furthermost dip,
which was wrapped in cloud. There were eyes on me. Then
I saw them. They were no more than three or four yards
away. They were set close together, in a hare's face,
brown, bright, almond-shaped. There was no intelligence
in them. I felt they were my eyes, staring down at Ishbel,
concentrated with an evil energy, and yet they were
staring at me. I felt as if the hare had sprung onto my
chest and was crouching there with heavy feet.

While the eyes were on me I saw myself holding
Ishbel under the water. The brown water of the burn
made partings over her face, like waving hair. Her face
was very pale. Her eyes had slipped out of her face and
there were only white circles, like snail slime. She didn't

move, after the first flutterings. A small trout darted from a round hole under the bank. There were wild nasturtiums growing above her head, bright orange and yellow, with their spotted, orchidaceous lips, and they made a crown over her head. The trout lay as if stunned by the giant's face under the water, then it went quick as a blink back under the bank again.

But all I did in effect was throw a stone. The hare went off on a slow bounce as I stooped to reach for a three-cornered stone from the crumbling wall. The hare looked quite domestic from behind, hindquarters low and rather fat. It didn't turn once, to give me the brown stare. I stepped out from behind the tree, raised my arm, and threw the stone as hard as I could at Ishbel.

> Take me to the station
> Put me on the train
> I got no expectations
> To pass through here again

The men are singing in the film. It's a desolate countryside, on the border with East Germany. It looks like most industrialised countries now, as if it's been made for passing through—yet where to? Piranesi's dreams have been realised, in an infinite complex of overpasses and autobahns. One of the men leaves the lorry and squatpees on a mound of industrial waste. Water trained for our uses sits in a square tray, about one hundred feet long, beyond the mound. Soon they will travel on, holding the only unchangeable thing left to them, reels of edited film.

It's a country of loss, where there's no point in mourning.

The stone hits Ishbel on the side of the face. Immediately several things happened. My mother ran out of the back of the house, skidded on the wet grass and threw herself at Ishbel, as if trying to shield her from me, too late. Ishbel's mother, who has just extricated herself from the jeep, stood back with a terrified expression, gazing up at the fringe of trees where I was hiding. The men, who were slithering down the bank to the picnic quarters, noticed nothing. It was only when they looked back— where was the rug, where were the women and the food— that they saw Ishbel still on the same spot with her hand held to her face. Her/my father climbed up the bank to comfort her. She pointed at the bracken at the foot of the trees. Yes, she was right! Ishbel knew where I was. Only she would know the exact place. Her mother, who had recovered herself by now, patted her cheek with a handkerchief. Was there blood? The bracken was too thick for me to see. Would they hunt me? I lifted my head a fraction in the hard fronds. Now I saw my mother and her mother together. What had I done? My mother was standing with her head to one side and she was pulling, pulling at her hair as if she was trying to get it out by the roots. Ishbel's mother was staring at her, for the first time she was taking a really good look, she could even afford to have her hands on her hips like a caricature of a fishwife, for my mother's child had thrown a stone at hers. And as she stared, my mother tugged at her hair and stood silent.

In the end, they did nothing. They ate the picnic, and threw the wine bottles and the beer cans down the bank, and packed up the greaseproof paper in the hamper. They went up to their holes in the side of the hill. Ishbel and her mother drove home in the jeep. But by then I had crawled through the bracken all the way along the hill. I was miles from where they were shooting, shivering and frozen, lying by a cairn on the highest, barest mountain above the loch which was fed by our burn. I could hear the shots. It was nearly dark by the time I limped home.

The film is over. I leave the cinema, knowing Ishbel is just behind me. In the foyer I turn quickly, to catch her there, but she is too quick for me, she has gone. I walk out into the real street. The buses are painted silver for the jubilee of the monarchy, the streets are as grey as the film I've just seen. Images from the real world super-impose on the film, and on Ishbel, my shadow, who must be following me somewhere—or I am following her?

GALA LIVES IN a messy ground floor flat in North London. There are wooden steps going down off a shaky wooden platform into the garden, the wood is grey with damp and age and the whole construction looks like some kind of underwater gallows, the packed, dense greens of the bushes and grass rising up to meet the feet of the suddenly falling victim. Cats with magpie markings prowl the low brick walls. There is nowhere less private than these gardens, which are overlooked by all the rear windows of all the houses in the street, yet oddly enough the patch of rough grass behind Gala feels completely secluded, as if she had cast a spell of invisibility on her minute portion of land. Because it was a warm day, and most of the families in the street were inside eating their Sunday meat, we took rugs out into Gala's garden and settled on the grass. I immediately asked her what she thought of my experiences of the last twelve hours.

Gala took some time to answer. She is a sculptor, her face is long and high-boned at the same time, like a stone face, a face from the desert, and her black eyes swim fiercely towards each other but at a downward angle, carried by a strong current for they flash and leap, even

when her face is at rest. A part of Gala has for a long time
been with Meg. She lives in fear, I think, of losing touch
with the spirit world, the world she needs for her work,
and of finding herself on the surface again, condemned to
tread endlessly the flat plains of accepted reality and
received ideas, her idea of hell as I suppose it would be
mine. But this doesn't mean she is incapable of being
realistic: her boyfriend Paul, who has a wife and children
in the country and is also a sculptor, is seen very clearly by
Gala: she is caustic and affectionate, and good at keeping
a distance in a situation in which she might well feel
miserable. Sometimes I think she does feel miserable more
often than she admits—but she has a good, strong laugh
and a love of the absurd. Also Gala, with her brittle bones
and her thin hands that look as if they could be unscrewed
at the wrist, is strong and tough. I know she may well be
stronger than I am. For the first time since she took me to
see Meg again, and I saw the first avenues of my escape,
I began to wonder if I had been right to go. It could well
be that Gala could cope with these other worlds as well as
the one in which we were sitting now—where the black
and white cats were jumping along the tops of the walls,
and a man in a short-sleeved shirt was standing heavy
with concentration at his kitchen window in front of a tin
and a tin opener, and his arm, thick with reddish hairs,
turned like a torturer's above the tin, and a plane above us
left a gap of white smoke on the sky—I couldn't. What
horrifying, uncontrollable regions might I find myself in
—perhaps forever? I told Gala of the waterfront at the
end of the High Street, and of my instant knowledge of

Ishbel. I was afraid. My hands were twisting on the edge
of the rug, and I saw Gala see them.

"You're looking for something," Gala said in a very
quiet voice. "It's not as simple as escape."

Gala gave a sudden smile as she said this. I wondered
how her voyages had affected her way of seeing her life.
She didn't seem very calm as a result of them: in fact she
was often nervous and agitated. But perhaps she would
have been unable to survive without her strayings into the
first circles of the outer world.

"Let's go in and have something to eat," Gala said.
"I'm hungry. No, Jane, it just sounds to me as if you've
got to do something about this sister Meg seems to have
given you."

"Do something about her? What do you mean?"

We were standing in Gala's kitchen now, after coming
up to the wooden platform and stepping from the damp
green garden into the clutter of indoors: enamel pots and
pans with half the enamel scraped off, an angular sculpture
by Paul, cushions and basketwork chairs. It was a relief to
be in. Gala took ham and some gherkins from the fridge
and reached over my head for plates.

We sat at the kitchen table. Gala was also a teacher, to
earn enough money to be independent of Paul, and exercise books were scattered on it, as depressing somehow
in their anonymity as faces of the unknown dead in
Eastern cemeteries: all the effort, the desperate upright
writing, and the feeling of seeing something that's not
meant to be seen. Gala pushed them to the far end of the
table. We began to eat.

"I hate correcting their work," Gala said with a half nod, for she must have known what I was thinking. "If I give them bad marks I feel low for days."

"And how's Paul?" The effect of the ham, and thick slices of white bread was to make the shadowy other life more doubtful, more distant. Gala shrugged.

"He's feeling old. He tells me that if his wife had been a more organised person he would have been a sculptor of the first class instead of the second. Presumably he tells his wife this too. It must be very irritating for her."

"It does sound very irritating." I laughed. "But you feel free of all that kind of thing, then?"

"Only because I never married or had children. I think it was because I can't bear criticism! It was built into the puritan idea of the family, I suppose. The head of the family may criticise the wife and the children. He may morally disapprove of them. Now why should anyone morally disapprove of me? I would lose my nerve as a sculptor if I were under a constant barrage of criticism!"

"Quite right," I said. I felt cheered up. Sometimes Tony's disapproval of me was as strong in the flat as the scent of a fox. It half choked me, I had to get out. It was strange, I thought, that Gala had two sides like this, and that I always forgot one when she turned to the other. But now she was reversing—after her loud laugh and a swig from the bottle of red wine on the table she fell silent again.

Her everyday thoughts began to be submerged and a

parallel track shot out ahead of them, going at a dizzying speed. I looked round the kitchen, feeling trapped. I wanted to go home. I would make it up to Tony, by cooking an evening meal, sitting in front of TV and watching old movies. But the thought of that was trapping too: they were eerie, the old, unageing stars acting out the fantasies of their long-dead scriptwriters. And the documentaries on 'thirties fascism, the faded goosestepping and deafening noise juxtaposed with brightly coloured food and bouncing pets, were more of a dictatorship of my mind than the travels imposed by Meg or Gala. I wondered how Tony could stand it. But he did more than stand it, he consumed it and helped to produce it. He moved freely in those wildly fluctuating zones of time and space.

"Give Meg a chance," Gala said. She got up and I followed her into the sitting room next door, which gave out onto a balcony too narrow to sit on and a low wrought-iron railing and the base of a thick tree with new green shoots sticking out from the bark. I saw that Gala was tired. When she sat I stood, my eye on the door.

"I think she'll help you to eliminate that bad sister," Gala said. She yawned suddenly and briefly, like a cat. Her eyes closed. She could sleep like that, anywhere and in front of anyone. But her expression, even when sleeping, was sombre. I wondered where she had galloped off to now. "Goodbye, Gala," I said in a whisper. I let myself out of the flat. And I went into the street feeling dejected and alone. All the excitement of last night had evaporated, and I wanted only to sit at home and think of nothing at all.

I wasn't really surprised to find her in the street. She was waiting by the corner. I had already passed several girls who could have been her: white face, empty eyes, dark hair. Now she had no name. She followed me to the bus stop and when I got on she hopped on last, as if she had only just made up her mind that this was where she wanted to go. She sat two rows behind me. I only dared to turn once, when asking for my fare. She was half obscured by a large African woman with carrier bags in a mountain on her lap. Was this half-hidden girl what Ishbel had looked like? She seemed a complete stranger, and utterly familiar at the same time. Her face gave no glimmer of recognition. Yet when we were there, at my stop, she got off ahead of me and I had to follow her all the way down the street to the block of flats.

As I went in I could feel my heart pounding. She had gone off down the street a little way and stood watching me with her back against the area railings of the house next to Paradise Island. A man came between us, heaving a crate of soft drinks. I ran into the cold, numb smell of the lino hall and jabbed the light button. I prayed that Tony would be in. I heard no steps as I scratched round my purse for my key. If she was there, she had come in silently and was standing still in the entrance to the hall where I couldn't see her.

The door opened. I pulled the key out clumsily and banged it shut behind me. The lights were on. TV voices spoke earnestly and then with laughter from the sitting room. I thought of the room empty, and the voices speaking to the empty room. I couldn't feel that Tony was there.

He was. He hardly looked up as I came in and threw myself down beside him. He was merged with the set, part of the antique dramas dancing in front of his immobile face.

I took his hand. I strained for noise other than that noise which seemed inescapable but could be cancelled at the click of a button. I wouldn't be able to turn this girl off at the switch. But it seemed that she hadn't followed me in after all. I could sense the complete silence in the other parts of the flat which always seems to reign when TV is on and claiming our attention, as if, transported somewhere else by the pictures, we are really no longer there and it can relapse into the silence of emptiness.

Tony gave me a quick glance. He asked me how I was. I said I was fine. Later he would ask me about the West German film, in two programmes' time probably. Slowly, sitting beside him there, I grew calmer. But it was always with the sense of being a victim that I went through the rest of the evening: I cooked dinner guiltily, I smiled at Tony too much and felt already that he had abandoned me, gone off—and rightly—to someone else. I was no longer the triumphant predator, I was persecuted and at fault.

The evening seems to last forever. Tony, who is good at suppressing his feelings but unable to prevent himself from showing triumph, came into the kitchen as I cooked the joint we should have had for lunch and ran his fingers through my hair. I saw us reflected in the window—it was growing dark at last—my hair standing up in hedgehog prickles and him behind me like a husband in an ad. They'd never let a woman with hair like that on the screen. And what were we advertising? Certainly not the quality of our life together—it was a long time since either of us had made the effort to understand what the other wanted. It was as if there was a limited space in our minds that was open to the other's mind, and the space was gradually closing.

"Hair still looks funny," Tony said. He tweaked it again and I winced. I made myself smile. Now! I said to myself. Go to the window and look. While Tony's here. Go on.

I went to the window, half-pulling Tony behind me, as if in an affectionate, playful mood. There was my face, coming up closer to me in the glass. There was the street, which only last night I thought I had left for the last time. I saw a straggle of women going into Paradise Island. Their jeans made a clot of darkness against the pavement. The moon was full but not yet strong. It hung above my reflected face: two round, foolish faces staring down blandly at the women below.

"Are you looking for the pots of herbs that used to be on the window sill?" Tony said. "Because they died. I threw them out this morning."

He sounded friendly and co-operative. It probably had been a boring day for him. I didn't answer, but opened the window and leaned out. He was still holding my hand, and he gave a surprised squeeze at my behaviour.

She was under the street lamp opposite. I couldn't see her eyes because they were in shadow, a shadow so deep that it looked as if she had empty sockets, as if the blackness on the upper part of her face were really night. She stood, as Meg had stood under the thin birches behind the cottage on Dalzell land, defiant and still—but this shadow owned all the world round her, by throwing her darkness over it . . . Margaret . . . my Meg . . . and my mother, is this what you've given birth to? She was like a woman who has been drowned in daylight, the lower part of her face as white as the day that saw her go. She was one of the women on the raft of the Méduse. She was gazing at me apparently sightlessly, with utter anguish.

"I didn't throw them out," Tony said, with good-natured impatience. "Is that the kind of thing you think I get up to when you're not here—throwing pots onto the heads of harmless passers-by?"

I drew back from the window and shut it. I was trembling, but Tony didn't seem to notice. When he was using his bantering tone he was particularly impervious to me.

I made the onion sauce to go with the meat. Tony stood at the sink, peeling potatoes. The meal would never be ready. It would never be eaten. I didn't know how I would make my body ingest it—and if I did, wouldn't it just sit there like a lump, for if time was refusing to move then the functions of the body would refuse to move too. How was she there? How did she dare to be there? The sky outside remained the same uncertain blue. We were in a perpetual twilight.

"So how was Gala today?" Tony said at his most jaunty. I knew he hated Gala. He suspected her of conquering me, colonising parts of me that couldn't be his. Not that he wanted them for himself, but it was irritating for him not to be complete possessor all the same.

"She was fine."

"Talk about anything interesting?"

"Oh, I can't remember . . . just the usual."

I wished suddenly that Tony *could* answer the questions I wished I had made Gala take more trouble over. What did she mean by my sister. My bad sister? How did she know about her, if Meg hadn't described what was going on? Or had she been there, watching me and Ishbel from behind a tree, shaping words out of our violence to one another?

"It must be lonely, being a sculptor," Tony said. I glowered at him: I was in no mood for fatuous remarks tonight.

Yet I laughed. The meal was before us at last, and Tony was eating with satisfaction. He put a blob of redcurrant jelly on the edge of his plate. He unscrewed a jar of mint sauce. He beamed down at his food. At last, as a recompense for having to wait for it, he was getting his Sunday lunch.

I glanced towards the window. It had grown darker after all. We were tilting away from the sun, we were spinning just as we always had done. The moon had grown stronger and more assured. I thought of Gala's face, pale on the cushions in her sudden sleep.

"It's time men were prepared to become more psychic," I said wilfully. "Then we'd be able to talk about the really interesting things—you know."

"I'm sorry, I'm sure!"

The lamb had put Tony in a benign state of mind. He cut himself another slice. The gravy was wrinkling already in the pan. The clock was ticking. She was standing out there, trying to jam the world into reverse. But it raced on without her, she stood under the moon like a sore finger. Would she be there when it was day? Day was waiting somewhere for her, a grey dawn standing in the swirling lino hall of my block of flats.

"Some things are too important to say," Tony said. "I wouldn't say them for anything."

TV. Coffee. I wouldn't wash up, in case I was tempted to look out at her again. Tony felt that by peeling the potatoes he had done enough. I felt his surprise when I sat beside him in front of the TV: he had unconsciously allowed himself a space on his own while I cleaned the kitchen. I was smiling at him, I was holding his hand, I felt his unease.

"Why haven't there been any great women composers," I said. "Why wasn't James Joyce a woman? Why are we so narrow in our minds and wide in our hips?"

The documentary was on Thailand. How did they manage to flatten the place like that. The people smiled despairingly at the camera, as the Americans had taught them to do. They knew they were revealing nothing, they glanced round uncomfortably, feeling the packaging coming down round them once more.

"Shall we catch some of Film Night?" Tony said.

The Thai vanished. I went into the kitchen after all. The night was still dragging. I poured out a glass of wine. I toasted my reflection, and the figure beyond, in the dark street. Idly, I opened the drawer of the kitchen table. The moon was shining right in at me now, and in Paradise Island they were dancing to revamped Elvis. Everything comes round twice, there's nothing new under the moon. I rummaged in the drawer, beyond the string and a worn ovencloth: my fingers were searching for something now.

It was so slow. After I found the photo I went back in to Tony with it. So there she was. The dark hair, the pale face. I recognised her straight away. The programme showed a clip from a Spanish movie—a woman was slaughtering a fox in a deep green stream by a millhouse. The green celluloid waves spurted jets of red.

"I've no idea how it got there," Tony said.

"But it's the one who was your girlfriend, isn't it?"

He sighed wearily. We were in a motor station in the States. There were two funny guys in the car. It was a comic film. Tony's stern mouth lifted in a smile.

"She's outside, waiting for you now. You never stopped seeing her, did you?"

"What on earth do you mean?"

"She's standing under the streetlamp. I recognised her at once."

Tony got to his feet. It was all so slow. He went to the

kitchen, he opened the window and leaned out. Later he chewed the back of my neck as we lay in bed. He came into me, but his body was dead. Had he really not seen her there at all? As in slow motion films, his cock moved in and out, paused, shuddered in an exaggeration of slowness, and released spray. The night was right over us now. Day was unimaginable. We lay breathing self-consciously, as if trying to catch each other out in some demonstration of lack of feeling. Had he really not seen her at all? Yet I knew she was waiting there for me.

I SLEPT AND I woke. The walls of the bedroom and the humps under the covers that were our bodies and the dim piles of our clothes on tables and chairs that looked as if they had come adrift from the floor were like characters in a forgotten language: if we could understand them— the four walls which man had for so long constructed for himself, the two bodies welded together by Nature's relentless urge, the familiar, perishable things which are kept for comfort—we would learn the world again, read the signs. But we've thrown down our blots. The image is more important than the real. The world swims beside its own satellite photograph, uneasily. And even in that room, where I had slept for years, there wasn't only myself and Tony. There was the photo of the girl. It lay two inches from my nose, on the thick shadow of the bedside table. I could see its white edges: she was preserved in four walls of white, as we were. I was sleeping between them—from time to time I turned to stare at the outline of Tony on the pillow and then back at her again. I picked her up delicately, by her corners, so as not to put my thumb on her face. Even in the dark I could see her, only her face looked paler and her eyes even more profoundly obscure.

I ached with loneliness. Tony's reptilian movements had done nothing to stir or assuage me. I jammed my fingers up against my cunt and pressed on the soft flesh. I wanted to make a gate there, never to feel the desolate openness again. My hand made a five-barred gate over the entrance. I saw the girl in flashes, riding Tony in a sexual frenzy, her pale composure gone. I saw them at a table, eating—outside was a green river and trees, they were enclosed in their privacy. Sometimes I saw her alone, and this was worse. She was quite self-contained. There was nothing in her screaming for a wild ride through the night. She fitted in the world like a glove. It protected her as she moved through it. She was quite complete in herself.

Jealousy. All this was quite untrue, of course. If she was half of me then she was incomplete, the half that was me she yearned for, her dreams of me were as much an invention as mine were of her. We envied and pitied each other, we begged for our fullness. Yet the joke in the whole matter was that these two halves were quite arbitrary—Tony, by needing us both, had split us in this way.

It wasn't a difficult thing to do. The Muse is female, and a woman who thinks must live with a demented sister. Often the two women war, and kill each other. I thought of the male Muse—or the male counterpart who is needed to make a woman complete in herself: he is yet to come. And as I lay hating the girl in the photo I wanted to expel her too, to throw her from my body. She had tormented me in childhood. She was always there, as she is now: with her secretive, slightly self-congratulatory manner that also suggests a passionate nature smugly concealed. She, my shadow who waits still in the street, is the definition of that vague thing, womanhood: a pact made with the eyes, signalled to men, that suggests women should pretend to enjoy a subservient position while ruling the men with 'an iron hand in a velvet glove'. Men like her because she is so finite. She never dreams, there is no static around her head—this is reserved only for me, only for the other sister, and in the terrible competitiveness, it's a battle she will always win.

The night shifted slightly, a grey bar showed under the door, but it would stay there a long time before it advanced. My mind moved too—through dates, meetings, moods: when had Tony last seen her, why had he placed the photo in the kitchen drawer? How long had it been there? I thought of my face hanging over the kitchen table, as I was chopping, skinning, peeling, plunging hands in flour only a tiny distance above that quiet smile, that dark head and white face. Did they do this together too—cook in her flat: did Tony stare at her hands kneading and wringing and coiling and straightening as dispassionately as he glanced at mine?

I crept up to Tony and touched his back, which was turned to me as always when he slept. He gave a grunt, a sigh. He had knowledge locked in him that could never be extracted. He was like a sealed pyramid: I wandered, lost in the labyrinth of speculations that lay around his inner knowledge. Yet, if he were really brought to account, Tony would probably be surprised at the idea he might love her more than me or the other way about.

There were as many strands to him, as there are to all of us, as veins in the body. Why did I feel I had to be the other half of him—or, for that matter, of the girl? Why this terrible need for joining, unless we were all perhaps two creatures once.

The restlessness couldn't go on. I knew from the implacable appearance of his back that Tony wasn't going to turn and hold me. I hated myself for only wanting him so ferociously because the existence of the girl had come to light again. I wondered if Meg had sent her, as a challenge. And I thought of Gala's words, that I should get rid of my bad sister.

It drove me mad, that she should be standing so patiently out there, waiting for Tony and me to come to an end, waiting to take him calmly from me. Only a short time ago I had been dreaming of my escape from him. Now she was there . . . she could wait as long as she liked but I would never lose either of them. Now—if I didn't let go—I had them both in the palm of my hand.

I got up and pulled on my skirt. I went to the kitchen, took the jeans and jacket out of the washbasket and substituted them for the skirt, which I threw in on top of Tony's musty-smelling shirts. The jeans went on without difficulty: as I lay in the dark bedroom I must have gone through my metamorphosis. I found my sandals in the corner of the kitchen. It was a warm night—warm in the kitchen, at least, with the cooker and the feeling of safety from the food, bread and spaghetti on the shelves. I didn't go to the window and look out, at the moon and the street lamp. Anyway, the moon had gone, risen, tugged away to a higher part of the sky. The light from the streetlamp came up at the window in a blue haze. I was going down the stairs, into the terrors of the hall, and out.

How bright it is. Even before I open the door I feel the brightness, which is trying to burst through the keyhole, and in at the hinges: a strong, white brightness, almost blinding. Day as it might be constructed by beings from a lightless planet after hearing descriptions of the pheno-menon: a force nine laboratory daylight. I half close my eyes before stepping out. This is day as you must remem-ber it when you are lying dying in the night. Day as white as ice and without shadows.

There are no signs of the street around me. I feel the block of flats at my back slip away like a heavy liner going down the estuary into the sea. Grass at my feet. Fields. Little flowers, yellow and white, which also look more invented or remembered than real—they are too neat, somehow, too well placed. I might be in a painting, or in a housewife's embroidered tea towel of the 'thirties, for a house with Jacobean chimneys, and a garden with dark red roses, and a reddish cow are all arranged straight on in my line of vision. There are no hills, and the width of the white sky is oppressive: it's like being under an eyeless head. Clumps of trees make an impressionistic fuzz behind the house. There is even a plume of smoke from one of the tall chimneys. What a comforting scene! How peaceful! I know I live there. But I hate it. I am afraid of it. Why do I have to live there? Why do I have to walk over the field, on a path conveniently stretching to a low stile, and then across the long grass of the outer garden, before sneaking through the roses to the back door. What crime have I committed, or am I about to commit?

I look down with dread at my body. The jeans and jacket I put on in the flat have disappeared and I see instead a black dress, about mid-calf length and of very poor material, and two impossibly white, floury legs, with mud marks on the ankles. My breasts are large, and in no way contained—they swing under the horrible dress at every step I take. I feel like a felon, a convict, a laughing stock. Have I just been publicly humiliated, pelted with rotten fruit in the village square, raped by the village idiot with froth at the corners of his mouth? I know I am reviled, hated. There is a great void in me, an O that drips and aches, a round sea with rancid tides that slap against me at the pull of the moon. But it's not a man I am looking for. I came out here in search of the pale girl with dark eyes. She is the only one who can save me. Without her I am too alone in this smug, tapestry world: I might die. She was waiting for me before. Now, when I need her so badly, she has gone.

In my cheap canvas shoes I can only walk slowly through the grass. It springs round my ankles and then back again, like a succession of feather traps. One of the strangest things about this landscape, I begin to see, is that although it gives an impression of such opacity it is in fact threadbare in places: there are tiny suggestions, as if the tea towel had got wet, worn thin, of the street where I live in London. For all the weight of the richness of the red land, and my body pulled like a sack to the well-settled house, and the woolly white sky, traces come through of the familiar pavements where I had gone in my jeans to seek the girl. Sometimes, underfoot, there is a fleeting glimpse of tarmac, a hardness through the thin shoes of broken concrete. In the fresh, untainted grass there lies a soft-drink can, such as are consumed at Paradise Island. And if I lift my head suddenly, a row of windows seems to appear in the sky, like an after vision from staring at a bright light: they turn to empty rectangles and are gone again. It feels, here, as if I have arrived in a place which is both the past and a piece of the future superimposed on the present. What I have done—what I am about to do—has been done, and until the balance of the world is restored it will be done again.

The uncertainty of the world where I am walking, despite its appearance of enduring stability, makes me feel more nervous and desperate than before. My thighs, fat and moist from the permanent, needing leak above them, smack together as I try to run, to reach the house. Surely she must be in there. She must be waiting for me there. But as I run I feel myself watched, pointed at, there is laughter. My breasts! My blubbery cheeks! To them I am an animal. Hardly worth feeding, let the fat sow lie on its side and die. But my arms at least have developed muscle. I have worked for them. I have heaved and hoisted. My thick back has a permanent pain from carrying for them. After the drunken dinners they come up the back stairs from the smoking room and into the bachelor quarters, and they rattle up into the attics, they want to stick themselves into my black swamp. But we have pushed the narrow brass beds against the door. We pant there, eyes bright with fear in the darkness. They go away from our pigsty muttering, to release themselves under plaster ceilings. They hate us, they see us as pigs.

Now I know why I have the feeling of being seen. I have reached the low stile and my legs open as I climb clumsily over it. They are playing tennis on a court just a few feet away, kept in by wire netting, running and leaping like prisoners in a cage, but it is they who are the jailers and those wandering outside who will never be free of their rule. One of them guffaws and points—specifically at my cunt, knickerless, exposed to them as I pant and clamber over the stile. They all pretend to drop their rackets and come after me. But the game is more important to them. I am over now, I head like a beast for the long grass, which parts to take me in on all fours, I run stooping through the moving flanks of grass. What will I do when I come to the rose garden? There is implanted in me already a memory, a prophecy, of punishment among the stiff roses, the violent movement of my body under a flogging beside the stiff, espaliered roses. I pause, my breath comes in short gasps. Kneeling in the furthest extreme of the long grass, I see my white, fat breasts heaving under the dress.

Of course! We're not allowed in the garden, my sister and I. Not in the formal garden. We would bring chaos, a bad smell in the place of the polite handkerchief smells this garden has been trained to produce. Yet sometimes we have to run through it—to deliver a message, to take food and drink at a sudden command to Master George, who makes a black pinch with finger and thumb on our legs. If we're caught, we're beaten. Even if we went the long way round, the gate from the drive is usually kept locked. So that's one of the ways they trap us—they'll beat us just for the sake of it. They whack out at us if they see us there with their flowers, they lash at us before the hedges clipped to the shapes of peacocks and chessmen— sometimes Master George is on the sitting room balcony and he laughs.

Still, I have to do it today. If I stretch my hand out I can touch the mown grass, the rolled lawn where we must not put our cheaply shod feet. It hardly looks like grass. It is so compressed it might be the filling of a sand- wich, with the earth they own below and the sky which is also theirs, fitting down neatly from above. All the daisies have been shaved away. I must go onto it, with my filthy legs and my unkempt, slobbering cunt, and crawl the length of the roses to find my sister.

The woman is coming down towards me from the direction of the house. She has a wide basket for flowers, secateurs and a hat tied down with a blue scarf to keep out the glare of their indigestible sky. Her eyes are tiny, triangular and blue. I know the coils of white hair she makes me brush at night. I know her artificial mouth, which she draws over the thin, unforgiving line of her own. There are dabs of rouge like pink sugar on her cheeks. But she is a death's head. In her stomach lie the small, permitted quantities of pastry and chocolate mousse and good meats served at their table in the light of white candles. She sees me, or rather she sniffs me. I can see her small, thin nose going up in the air and a small, detestable smile. I stay like an animal, resting on my hands on the mown lawn, which seems to melt, to dissolve under my weight. She comes up closer and stops.

"What are you doing there, Jeanne?"

"I was looking for Marie, ma'am."

"And why should Marie be in the rose garden, I wonder?"

"She was taking a cool drink to Master George, ma'am."

The woman looked down at me in complete contempt. She was tired today, there would be no floggings. But she leaned down with the secateurs and nipped my ear. I let out a scream. It sounded like a pig's scream. At the same time, through the woman's legs, I could see Marie coming. She was running down the path, her black hair out behind her, her horrible dress, exactly the same as mine, beautiful on her body. I moaned for her.

The woman turned and shouted at Marie to get off the path. So Marie came the last hundred feet plunging through the waving grass. She was electric, the grass hissed as she ran.

"Irish sluts!" the woman said. She left us, wandering down the path to the deepest red roses. Her hat was at a saucy, arrogant angle. I could have run behind her like a Japanese warrior, I could have jumped her from behind. She was so frail, half my size. But they owned everything. We were cramped, slave giants in their small, perfect world.

At last we were together. There, in the concealing grass, I searched her face anxiously. She was my sister, all my dark sisters. I had never needed her so much. I had never known her so well. We would never be enemies. We never had been. With our love for each other we would keep the rest of the world away.

We went the long way round, and climbed the locked gate. We crept in the back door, by the dark box hedges which smell of urine. The cook shouts at us—vague abuse.

Then we are up the back stairs, up and up against the brown paint worn to a shine by the backs and buttocks of beasts of burden, footmen and chambermaids and all those who wait on Mr and Mrs Aldridge and Miss Sylvia and Master George. All who serve the Manor and the enduring tapestry, although here and there it is wearing thin.

Our room, white and pointed, crammed under the eaves like a house marten's nest spattered with white shit, has two beds narrow as shoe boxes and a round window that looks out onto the central courtyard. Marie and I are in the one bed now, and our black dresses, which we never take off, even to sleep, are up around our waists. With our fingers we give each other comfort. We are kissing and biting. Her black hair is in my mouth. I will die, float, never let her out of my sight again.

MONDAY. TONY HAD a quick breakfast in the kitchen. I lay in bed. My body was aching, my back and thighs with pains like contractions, as if the expansion and shrinking they had undergone had simulated the labour pangs of my birth as another. I was more at peace. Tony had removed the photo of the girl while I slept, and I knew no one was waiting outside for me. Day takes away these shadows—sometimes at least. And my jeans and jacket were folded neatly on the bedroom chair, as if I had gone nowhere at all. These magic garments, which make you invisible because everyone wears them, which transcend sex and wealth and individuality—who had folded them like that when I came in?

Tony brought me a cup of tea in bed. I looked at him, wondering if I might ask. He sat down on the chair, on top of the jeans, and my heart missed a beat.

"Looks as if we might get the girl who plays Emmanuelle as Flora de Barral," Tony said. "She's very small and thin. It might be good."

Poor Flora, whose life was recounted by three men, all equally determined on her helplessness and fragility. If she had had power, she would have turned their words into meaningless gossip by taking matters into her own hands and doing something so unacceptable they would have been unable to recount it. But she was impotent: while they inveighed against the feminism of Mrs Fyne she meekly followed the destiny laid down for her. I smiled at Tony and nodded my head. He saw I was laughing, and frowned.

"Will she strip in the film?"

"Don't be silly. Of course not." Tony leaned forward and put his hand on my foot under the bedclothes. "Well . . . I've got to be off really. And I'm going to Milan tonight. For a few days. It's to polish up the script. It's just come up or I would have told you before."

"With her?"

Tony looked at me with what seemed a purposeful stupidity. His eyes were like a cow's—or I could see that was what he was aiming for. They were shallow and vague, pupils wandering, smooth as polished veneer. She was for a moment reflected in them: a minute figurine of her, she was standing with a hand on her hip, in a 'fifties skirt, and she was smiling like a hostess in a TV ad. I winced at her and looked away.

"Did you take her photo from the table here while I was asleep?"

Tony's voice was blurred in his new stupidity. "Honestly, Jane, I don't know what you're talking about. What photo?"

"The photo that was in the kitchen drawer. For God's sake, Tony, don't start pretending it wasn't there." I sat bolt upright. My thighs, stretched as bows made from wet wood, ached beneath me. I was weak today. Why did he have to go like this? My eyes filled with tears.

"Oh, that. I'm not pretending it wasn't in the kitchen drawer."

"Well, never mind."

What did it matter? I had my film review to write. I would go and see Stephen when I had finished it, he would calm me like a familiar blanket. For if Gala travelled sometimes too far, to the dangerous limits of the mind, Stephen remained always within the same ground. His ground was less tenable than hers—he was training to take Holy Orders, he 'believed', and Gala would never understand what that could mean. But his madness was sanctioned, worn as cloister stones. Paradoxically, his belief in something unprovable and unseeable only seemed to confirm the reality of the palpable world. When I was with him I drank tea and whisky and ate biscuits and felt the small comforts and irritations of childhood. One of his rugs was scratchy to sit on. His mugs were chipped. When I thought of him these things returned to me intensely, physically.

"I won't be gone long." Tony smiled and patted my foot. I moved it away clumsily, it felt as heavy as if it were wrapped in plaster. "Jane, give us a kiss, then. And I hope your hair grows!"

How charming Tony could seem! He stooped over me like a handsome doctor and his lips made a bulbous shape as they came closer. His eyes were still blank, and his lips were like the magnified image of an insect's eye, popping pink membrane, blind but feeling, probing. I met them. They were warm and opened up further, to a shelf of saliva and then blackness. They went into a final smile before he left.

"Don't see too much of Gala! OK?"

Then he was gone. Tony wasn't as much of a fool as I —and he when it suited him—thought. He knew something. Just as surely as I knew the girl was still in his life, still part of his flesh, crawling in his arm hairs, moving in the packed cranium which must contain so many memories of her. I would always know this, however much he denied it. And now he knew about Meg. Perhaps he thought of Meg, but he had only seen her once. And for a time I lay back in bed, thinking of the girl, and killing her atom by atom inside me, tearing and fading her image until she was no more than a floating negative print in a pool of developing liquid, black as dark red blood. The dim light went out and I saw nothing. For a time I slept. When I woke, it was to realise that Tony had properly gone, and that I was alone.

I posted my review on the way to Stephen's. I was glad to be out of the flat. Once the feeling of Tony had gone, the shadows made themselves felt everywhere: Ishbel behind the doors as I opened and shut them in my nervous hurry, Marie in the kitchen, sticky and warm. And the girl, Tony's girl, was mocking there somewhere. They had taken over the place—it was as if, since my first journey and thwarted escape, they considered me out of this world and themselves, my ghosts, the legitimate heirs. I thought I wouldn't go back until Tony returned. I would stay with Stephen—or with Gala perhaps. Then I thought of Stephen's spare room, its absolute colourlessness, the sense when confronted by the faded chintz bequeathed by his calm mother of a nothingness in the world filled by polite chatter, herbaceous flowers, newly baked cakes which already contained the smell of their staleness, and I knew I would go and see Meg. In Stephen's world, so much had been brushed under the carpet that although he hadn't lived the life of his parents for years, some of it was still his: sudden moments of embarrassment with him would come from the rush of involuntary thoughts, which all this concealment in his past made inevitable. The deadly, 'good taste' Persian rugs brought pictures of women of fifty struggling to keep their heads above water, their blouses buttoned at the wrong button over rasping, red chests. The stiff Dutch tables were his father in the bathroom, a rustling newspaper, a bad gut, the lawn mower going outside as a life of dividend-supported, uneventful failure went by with the shit. Stephen was unaware of the climate of his house. But I couldn't sleep there now. And at Gala's it was trying to lie in another's spoor. There was no inch that she hadn't protectively covered with reminders of her worldly, and other-worldly identity: letters from solicitors, poems, childhood journals in different-coloured inks, hats with poppies stuck in the brim, long, spotted scarves. I would drown there. So I knew, by the time I got off the bus and walked up Stephen's street, that I would go and see Meg. I calculated I had three days before the next viewing of a film, and before Tony got back. In three days I might rise again. I could lose my shadows, and walk alone.

Stephen was in a white silk caftan, with bobbles swinging from the sleeves. He stood to greet me in his pale blue hall like a plaster madonna in a niche. He was plumper, and his gingery hair grew forward onto cheeks plump as a pigeon's breast, like pale flames threatening to consume the face. He was smiling, his small eyes were nearly shut. Stephen might be eaten, or licked, and he moved as if he knew this, like a tempting piece of food being jerked always just out of reach by an unseen hand. He gave off a smell of orange water. It was three or four years now since the conversion—when Stephen had decided to study to join the Church. He was horrified by pain and injustice, and it was true that in his presence it seemed impossible to believe in such things. Perhaps that was why he added so greatly to the physicality of objects and surroundings—when one was with him he and everything round him seemed the only reality. Yet he led a spiritual life, as well concealed as the crimes and sadness of his parents' life: he prayed, and fasted, and felt the existence of God.

"Have you been seeing that woman again?"

Stephen put his Jesus-robed arm round me and we went into the sitting room together. I flinched as I always did at first at the square chairs, the horticultural covers nibbled by long-dead dogs. I went to a sofa and went down with a bump. The ancient springs creaked beneath me. I had told Stephen about Meg, but some time ago. Now

I regretted it. Since then, I had travelled. He would be horrified by my journeys, though.

"Yes. At a party on Saturday night. She's sent me all over the place, Stephen. Don't ask me to give it up."

"Why should I ask you to give it up?"

Stephen looked surprised. There was a plate of cakes on the table, and a pot of tea. In heaven Stephen would have cakes and tea, as if resigned to an eternal station waiting-room.

"Have some tea," Stephen said. "But Jane, I'm not laughing at you—I'd like to know where you went. I've tried often, you know . . . to get somewhere, *anywhere* that would help me to understand the Divine mysteries. As so many doubters have said: just one glimpse of God and I'll be faithful for the rest of my life."

"This isn't about that," I said. "This is about believing something different."

Then I stopped. It seemed already that another voice had spoken from inside me. I mustn't find myself at war with Stephen now, when I no longer knew what I believed.

"You can hardly tell me you're going in for the fashionable demonology," Stephen said with a laugh. "An emancipated woman gives birth to the Devil! I've seen the movie."

Stephen was pink and fluffed when he was annoyed. I was frightened to see him like that, for it seemed I must have brought something in with me, a cobweb from the nocturnal branches of my walks. Did I seem changed to him, or utterly different? I had only seen Stephen like that once before, when we were in the park and a big boy had knocked a smaller one to the ground and stamped on his head.

"My clothes stink of sulphur when I get back," I said. I laughed—it was worth the risk. But I could feel my dark sister, my Bad Muse, stir inside me and object to my flippancy. However much I wanted to keep Stephen as a friend, I must not betray my new path. Of course—and here my heart sank—she was only speaking like that because she knew Stephen was one of the few people who could dissuade me from the course before it was too late.

"You might be possessed," Stephen said. He hadn't laughed at my reference to the sulphur. He looked serious. It occurred to me suddenly that he believed in all this kind of thing far more than I did, with God and Heaven and Hell. He might even think I had been to Hell. Perhaps I had.

"Can I have a cake? Listen, Stephen, I really don't think all this is to do with religion at all. I think it's to do with people having power over others—I think Meg can control the lives and thoughts . . . and invisible movements, if you like . . . of a lot of people. I think . . . that she wants people to learn about themselves, to see the world below the surface."

"I see," Stephen said. He watched me as I ate the cake, with his head to one side like a large bird. "And what are you supposed to give her in return?"

"Well . . ." I said. I felt uncomfortable. "Nothing as far as I know." I finished the cake, and looked at the last crumbs fall onto the Persian rug with the same fascination as I always felt at all the small manifestations of the ordinary in Stephen's flat. There was a silence between us, as I thought of Meg again. She was reversing science, translating the known into the unknown. With her power, the old magic that people had known would pour back into the world again. Because she believed so completely in her words, what she believed would come true.

"Are you still thinking about that girl of Tony's?" Stephen asked. I felt uncomfortable again: Stephen was too close on my heels today. Yet I should confide in him, tell him how the shadows were always there now, one of them the girl, and the others . . .

"Most of the journeys I've done have been penances," I said to Stephen. "Don't think I've been *enjoying* myself."

At this we both burst out laughing. It seemed ridiculous, even in a discussion on the possibility of a Second State, Another Reality, or whatever it might be called, that I was still anxious to give assurances of a bad time. The Puritan instinct is the hardest to die. And I wanted it to die, one of the reasons I would follow Meg wherever she sent me, for one day soon I would reach regions far removed from the Puritans and the black, clayey soil in which you must lie in unending suffocation for your sins.

"No, I don't think about the girl all that much," I said. I saw Stephen blink, he didn't believe me. "Tony doesn't see her any more, anyway."

"Oh, I thought you said he did." Stephen looked hurt. The last time we'd met I had told him so much, and now I was curt and offensive. Despite his enjoyment of our laughter he was sad again now. He took another cake, predictably.

"Why is the sea always connected with crime?" I said. I was thinking of the waterfront, where Meg had given me the first glimpse.

"And madness," said Stephen, giving me a quick glance. "The mad were put out to sea and they wandered rudderless. The ship might nudge into the coast of Holland and go up a canal. Think, if you were sitting in your garden . . ."

"Surrounded by tulips," I said, beginning to laugh again.

"And one of these ships came along the canal a few feet away."

"With men with striped caps and bells, and people whose bodies had quite gone and only eyes and hair remained . . ."

"The sea, mad and female, the criminal's punishment." Stephen shrugged. "An inspiration to kill, perhaps, from the depths of the irrational, from the waves that hide all traces. I don't know. Seriously, Jane, is that where she sent you?"

"Maybe."

Again I felt another voice had answered. Our enjoyment died away. I suddenly saw very clearly the sea on the South coast, when Stephen and I had gone on a day-trip once: a sea with blue ruled lines like a child's exercise book, not the sea I wanted, very short grass on the cliffs, flowers too painfully small, birds chirping. Stephen had brought the picnic. There were thick sandwiches, with slices of tongue. We had talked about nothing much. This would never happen again.

"Do you think I'm mad?" I said.

Stephen sighed.

"No, I don't. But I don't think you have any idea—either of what's going to happen to you or of what you're really looking for. Do you think the world is that bad? Do you really feel you must leave it?"

"I'm not going to leave it. I'm just going to understand it in another way."

"And another thing, Jane. You don't know what Meg is going to exact from you. You must be prepared to think about that carefully."

"My soul?" I smiled. "I haven't got much of a soul, Stephen, but she's welcome to it."

"Jane! That's a terrible thing to say."

All Stephen's recent conversion appeared on his face at that point. His eyes went upwards, his cheeks went a deeper pink, in his martyrdom, cake in hand, he gazed at the ceiling. I got up, fighting back a smile.

"I must go, Stephen. Thank you for the tea. That was nice."

"But you know it wasn't!" Stephen was on his feet, very agitated. "You've never been like this with me, Jane. You seem quite . . . you seem totally translated!"

Translated! It may have been a slip of the tongue. But that was what was happening to me. I was being translated into another state, without death to intervene. I was going from the known state to the unknown. I went up to Stephen very contrite and kissed his soft cheek. "I'm sorry," I whispered at him. "I'll see you soon. It'll be better then."

"Wait a minute!"

Stephen went to a cupboard in the corner of the sitting room. He rummaged about inside, his back large and womanly in the white robe. There were boxes of stationery and rolls of gift wrapping paper. He pulled something out and turned to come towards me with it.

Soon I saw what it was, although at first I couldn't make it out. It seemed to look like a rhinoceros's horn. But it was a crucifix, of course. It was made of imitation ivory and a small, faintly coloured-in Christ hung from its arms. There was a gold chain attached.

"Put it round your neck," Stephen said. He put the chain over my head. The crucifix dived down the front of my shirt and came to rest between my breasts. The coldness brought a shudder through my body. I looked down and saw the tiny Christ jigging there, cupped by mammary flesh.

"If . . . if you're frightened, Jane . . . why not use it?"

"Thank you, Stephen. You're very sweet."

We kissed. I walked down the blue hall to the door. I looked back once, for I knew Stephen would be standing there, his eyes rushing upwards and back again in anxiety. He gave a pretence of a light-hearted wave when he saw me turn. But he couldn't keep up the façade. By the time I had opened the front door, he was safely inside his sitting room again, wrapped in the wings of his robe, in his favourite chair by the cakes.

The air is very bright and pale outside Stephen's door. There are his front door steps, which have been scrubbed and rained on until they look like slabs of hard, dirty sugar. The bottom one dips in the middle. The maid-servants in their long black skirts wore it down as they trudged, in and out, out and in, the black pendulum of their labour and their unrequited lives, the pallbearers wore it down as they carried them out, the householders in their stiff hats pressed down firmly on the step: it was the boundary of their territory: it might go down under them but it would not move.

And yet the step is not so respectful as it was. The cement is cracked at the side, which makes the step un-steady, no longer so firmly anchored to the black railings, and this seesawing has in turn cracked the step itself. The fissure runs with violent twists and turns the length of the step. It's not very wide, but moisture has gathered there from past rains. I put both my feet over it and feel the tilt. The thin lips of the fissure are directly beneath me, and the globules of moisture like spit. I imagine that if I were sucked down into this aperture I would sink into the centre of the earth. There, in the hot brown earth along with the bowler hats and the dead maids and the starched aprons laid out in boxes, I would wander forever. I can see the labyrinth of passages, none more than a foot wide: like buried Rome, no elevation of the spirit after death but a dragging down into the bowels, a narrowing amongst the broken games and smashed mosaics and bal-loons hanging like young boys' painted faces in the lean-ing streets. I would go down into the world that had produced Stephen and his kind. The people and the prayers and the secret lives, layers of rich coal under the decaying house. From this hell there would be no escape. I would brush the earth walls of those terrible subterranean streets with wide skirts, bleeding onto discreet rags, giving birth in agony in mud caves hung with rich hangings, dying with my child on linen bedding—I would never rise away from it. I would be remodelled when I was needed again—prostitute or maid or wife with bombazine and keys. There was little sound down there. No one would hear my cries.

So I stood on the step a while to gain my balance. It rocked gently beneath me. I closed my eyes. I could see the haunted eyes of the people as they came and went on the pavement. What happened to them? Did they go out of their houses one day and find themselves seized by eagles, carried to an eyrie from which they could look down on the wickedness and deceit of the world, see it written in the serpentine rivers and the ranges of mountains like gnashed teeth, and the swamps and rain forests that dragged you in and left you there—had they returned without their illusion, with starved eyes? I could hear a bunch of children coming in my direction along the street. At least they didn't know, or care. They were jumping over the cracks in the pavement, while I still stood on the crack in the step. Perhaps it was the origin of the game: they knew hell was waiting for them between the paving stones.

The step, very gradually, increased the seesawing motion. It was pleasant, like being in a boat going at a stately pace across a lake. The fine white light came down on my face and my upturned, closed eyelids. If only life was always like this! I had all the time in the world. When I was rested, I would go and see Meg.

I thought of my life, and the surface where I live with Tony, and the hard, bright entrances to the modern cinemas where I go to watch the mushy, coloured dreams of the future. Those mirrors aren't worth walking through. I thought of Stephen and the vision of Heaven he carries in his head. I thought of the crucifix he had given me. But I could no longer feel it against my skin: it had assimilated itself with me, and wherever I went it would have to go too. I wondered, standing there, suspended in time, what Meg would do for me when I saw her. I could feel, now, that my shadows had been removed and that I was allowed to sample, for a while, the feeling of completeness. It was as if she had given me something else in place of the bad sister, something that made me as strong and round as the beginning of the world. For this feeling, I knew I would give her anything she asked. I was an addict already, dreaming on the white-grained step, emptiness blocked out. My sisters had been nightmares. Meg would help me to drive them away, black bats of uncertainty and loneliness and despair. I would walk on my own and in my own place so that not even the strongest wind could blow me down. I knew Meg wanted to take, in return for this, everything I had: my salvation would be paid for in blood, but never hers: she was anti-Christ, she would take where he gave, the wooden cross on which he hung, a passive victim, she would plunge into the heart of her prey. That was the first time, as I stood swaying there on the tilting step between the two worlds, that I understood what she was and where I was going. I understood the meaning of the sacrifice, that I would be a living shadow, a walking living being without a shadow, a drinker of blood, a nightwalker in perpetual and thwarted search of day, a white skin without blood, a dark predator, a victim. I knew I would be lured to this by the promise of the journeys, and the final ecstatic completeness: I saw that Stephen and Gala both knew it and were afraid for me. But I could no more turn back now, with one foot stretched forward into the magic, invisible current of air that would carry me on, and the other on the fissure in the step, holding down the bonemeal of the past, than make myself forget the journeys I had already undertaken. I was committed. I had never been committed before. The people on the pavement, with their starved eyes and their TV, believed in nothing. Yet there was an irony in believing that I would be happier, or superior to them, when I had gone over to Meg. For my eyes would be starving too. I would hover over them in my endless quest for the feeling which Meg would occasionally allow me. A junkie with no eyes flitting behind trees. They would shrink from my touch, from my gravebreath. An upright shadow, draining life. Still, I wanted to go on. The white light bathed my senses, in my absolute happiness I swore I would go on.

The step broke off the seesawing movement, and the abrupt stopping sent me down onto the ground. It was like walking off a merry-go-round at the fair, I felt dizzy and the ground spun as I opened my eyes.

Stephen's street had disappeared. I was in a forest, which was dappled with light and shade, so much so that the proportions of darkness and light seemed exactly right: small clouds raced over the portions of the sky that were visible, exactly corresponding with the delicious patches of shade on the ground under the trees; pale gold and green grass was as light as wheat in the sunlight, and cushions and banks of moss as deep green as if they had been saturated with water from an underground spring. Birds were flying about in the forest. They were black and bright blue and their song was harsh. Where they flew the forest changed, into a blue metal forest, without the light and the shade. In those parts of the forest where they flew I could see wolves, and sometimes a movement like a figure in the trees. In that part of the forest the trees were as straight as metal, and without shadow. The wolves never stopped pacing, under a sun unfiltered by leaves.

Where I was, however, seemed to me the most beautiful place I had ever seen. The black and blue birds never flew into the part of the forest where I was standing— they stopped short, always, on the other side of a small round clearing, a kind of fairy ring, some distance away. There was a stream a few feet in front of me, and it too was dappled evenly, like tortoiseshell. White flowers— Solomon's Seal and Star of Bethlehem—grew under the light, graceful trees, which had bark spotted dark and light as a leopard's back.

I sat down by the stream and picked some of the white, bloodless flowers. I felt balanced, contained by the shade as if this place, this forest, was the most perfect combination of the world's beauties, at the same time bright and obscure, warm and cold, concrete and hallucinatory, like the forest on the other side of the clearing, the hard minerals at the core of the world, and the hunger and evil walking the streets. The world was all around me, in its unchangeable balance. I looked down at my body, and saw how the chameleon dappling moved to accommodate the white flowers I held against my dress, and the dark shadow made by my head tilting down. The light and shade flowed endlessly, like film, the essence of illusion, positive and negative light.

When I looked up again I looked directly at the clearing. There was something there. The sun and the leaves had become agitated in their patterns on the ground. The symmetry of the carpet was disturbed. And the walls of the clearing, the silver birches tainted with gold, knobbles protruding on the bark like bruises on the moving, swaying trunks, seemed to have closed ranks behind the clearing, to be shutting out the hard forest beyond. I rose and walked slowly towards the clearing.

The figure in the middle of the ring was hard to see, for the light and the goldness and the darkness played over him continually. He seemed to be wearing a coat made of shadow and light, of reflected leaves and pinstripe of bark, a patchwork of sylvan colours. His head, blindingly clear at one moment in the flashes from the sun, would vanish, and then change again. He was tall, but only as tall as the

bolt of the sun that fell over him—when the leaves overhead rustled and changed he disintegrated into an
autumnal chaos before reassembling in the mossy ring.

I walked up to the edge of the circle. A thin haze of
light like a mesh wall kept me from going any further. I
saw him as he stood before me, as he melted into striped
and filmy air and came back into split second focus. He
was extraordinarily like me. I felt that sense of recognition
and disbelief which jars at the sight of an unexpected
mirror: the thing before you that is too familiar and too
strange. But I knew him. I reached out my hand, and the
light and shadow fell evenly on my arm, making gold
bars on the dusky, dim skin. He smiled: I saw him clearly
then. But before I could speak a wind that soughed like
an evening wind came down over the trees around us.
The branches were tossed as if a hand had come up from
below and squeezed them into a broom to scour the sky.
They sighed and rattled, and as they divided, the even-
ness of the light and shadow was gone, and he disappeared. He might have flown up one of the shafts of
white air in the parted trees. Or he might have gone into
the ground, like a fox. The light in the ring was flat, and
tired—round a tree stump there was a slight enhancement,
from the dying goldness of the day, and a sense of shadow
on the moss. I went to sit there. I was disconsolate.

Some time passed, which could be seen as a gradual
blindness, for as I sat on in the abandoned circle the
range of what was visible grew less and less, and I felt
the light as it faded was coming directly from my eyes. It
was twilight: the balance of two lights—the grey sur-

render of the day to the pounce of the night—but the balance I had known in the bright gold of the forest was gone. I felt completely alone. Where had he gone? What had he meant? And how would I ever reach Meg, now that strips of black cloud as wide as shawls were coming down on the deepening grey over the trees? The silver birches were becoming white. The bruise patches on the trunks looked like the faces of small animals, tucked into their sides for the night. My body ached with loneliness. My fingers and toes tingled like quicksilver, as if some message from somewhere were urging me to run before it was too late.

In the metal forest, a melodramatic Disney-movie night had set in. And I could see her waiting for me there, under a hard moon bright as a sequin, by the straight trees which looked as if they had just been sprayed with aluminium paint, her head to one side and her eyes as always in deep shadow. He had gone, and she had returned to me. She was my curse, my bitter dragging-down weight that would keep me out of true all my life, pulling one side of me down in grief and rage, snapping my heart. The wolves walked round her, but they didn't turn to look at her. She was all mine, she was for no one but me.

I rose and walked out of the ring. I left behind the twilight, the uncertain time when the world might turn and go in the other direction. Meg had sent me the vision. I thought of it as I walked straight into the metal forest. I walked past the girl, who was leaning against a tree, her lips blue in the unnatural light from the moon. I went on, through the lines of trees as straight in rows as the crosses of dead soldiers. I looked back once and she was following me. Meg had sent me the vision. I would lose her in the end.

There was no way of measuring time in that artificial forest. My heart beat as if it could hardly beat any longer. My legs felt nothing. After a time, through the last rows of the trees, I saw the lights of Meg's house.

MEG'S HOUSE WAS in one of the streets allowed to remain 'pretty' in Chelsea. The houses were low, and flanked by magnolias. The doors were painted fruit colours. Rock music on summer nights was subdued here; the crowds, the mixing of the races, the energy and the corruption and the optimism and despair of modern London were kept out by a system of one-way and dead-end signs more potent than written language. This timelessness—chi-chi is the word that would have been used to describe it a quarter of a century ago—was odd and disconcerting. Even the young people seemed to wear deliberately dated clothes. Posters of the Queen were on show in several windows. There was an air of slightly self-conscious well-being as if the residents knew they were exhibits, perhaps: last traces of a vanishing way of life. My shadow, with her shoulders hunched in a black coat, and her sallow face and her black, sightless stare, was horribly out of place here. She turned the corner after me, and leaned against a low wall as I rang at Meg's bell. She looked like a mur-derer, or a rapist. As I waited for Meg, I watched women cross the street rather than walk into this sudden chilling patch of shade.

The patio in front of Meg's house was whitewashed, and there was even a grape vine climbing a neat canopy of trellis over the porch. The windows had muslin sash curtains, tied, Bo Peep style, with shiny blue ribbons. The house looked blind, and white, and innocent—a nest for an old woman with fleecy hair, a retreat that was at the same time a fashionable and expensive investment. It had all that disingenuousness. That was why, I remembered, I had shuddered at it when Gala took me there—for finding Meg inside was like opening a mother-of-pearl box and finding inside a jet of fire.

Meg opened the door. Along the street, my sister moved restlessly. It was a bright day, and she wanted the unmitigated black of the forest, or at least the two lights of evening, to help her creep up on us. A light wind stirred the flowers and leaves outside the neat houses. And a sweet smell came off them—it may have been lime—it was the sweetest I had ever known. I wondered, when we were in Meg's narrow hall, why she chose to keep it out and burn the inevitable incense sticks. The heavy, Eastern smell closed us off from the street more effectively than thick curtains. I could sense my shadow moving closer, pressing up against the impenetrable scent.

Ah, it was a relief to be in! To be in there, in the red glow. Meg kisses me on the cheek. She looks amused. She is in a long gown of deep red, slashed at the bosom to show a white neck like a column going up to support a Roman head. There is a band of cherry velvet round the middle of the column, and a white rose pinned under her left shoulder. Her lips are carmine, and glisten under the soft red lamp from the hall ceiling. She doesn't take my hand, but leads the way to the first floor sitting room. It is redder than I remembered, the light so red that it becomes grains of redness, like African sand in a sandstorm. You can almost touch it. We sit on the pile of cushions, by the claw-legged table with the red baize cloth.

"I've shown you a great deal," Meg says. "How have you liked it, Jane?"

She must know. She must know very well why I am here. Yet I hold back, as if afraid to answer. Meg's head is tilted to one side, like a statue decapitated at the cherry velvet band—down one side of her face runs a shadow of the deepest red.

"I . . . I want to go back to the waterfront. Why can't I go back there, Meg?"

"The waterfront?" Meg chuckles. "You want to leave on the ship, you want to go there again?"

"No . . . I . . ."

I am becoming confused now. Meg's tones are distant and rather affected, as if I had disturbed her in preparation for one of the soirées common in the area. I see there are candles—red of course—burning on the card table at the end of the room. A scarlet-headed Tarot card lies on the top of the pack there. Perhaps she really is planning to entertain. I came at the wrong moment. I can feel my triumphant shadow stir outside in the street, just under the trellis of vines.

"Of course you shall go there again. But perhaps not quite yet, Jane!" She reaches out both hands, and places them over mine. As happened when she did this last time, I feel astonishingly refreshed: my fear begins to slip away.

"That's better," Meg murmurs. "My poor Jane! What you've been through! My poor Jane! And that girl such a tiresome nuisance to you . . . inside you day and night, enemy or friend, enemy shadow . . . or sister . . . I've seen her . . . she dogs you day and night. Oh yes . . . I know. And only when you are rid of her will you go to the port again . . . and see the man . . . the man in the clearing in the forest, you know . . . Oh yes, he'll be there, Jane. How would you like to be with *him*, instead of *her*? Ah, it's hardly a question, is it?"

Meg breaks off at this point and looks with such intensity in the empty grate that I fancy she has started a fire flickering there—for a second I see the orange, leaping flames and a face, a face of forked flame, a face that is my own and looks straight into my own—then it is gone and the stifling red of the room closes in on us once again.

"Certainly you can't live with them both!" Meg gives a short laugh, rises, and pulls me up with her. "It's so easy, Jane. Get Tony's girl, bring her to me, and I'll do away with the rest of them, I promise you!"

"Get Tony's girl?"

All the while, with her light hands, Meg is pulling me across the room and out onto the landing. I see the door into another room I had never noticed before is open to receive us. A slice of reddish brown light comes out at us on the gloom of the landing, like the blade of a rusty knife. I hang back, heavy as a stone, afraid.

But Meg drew me through the door into the room. My palms were ice cold now, and wet, but Meg's touch was unchanged. I looked round the room, which was as dim as the sitting room, and small, although it was difficult to tell the proportions in the infra-red glow. There were glass cabinets, and files; in the far corner, pushed up against a heavily curtained window, was a divan covered with a patchwork quilt in diamond scarlet and white pattern. Meg slid open the top of one of the show tables and pulled out two squares of glass with a coil of hair between. I turned to search for the door, which had closed behind us and was now invisible in the small, square room the colour of dried blood. I was in panic. Meg held the twist of hair up close to me. It lay inert and brown as a long-dead caterpillar between the miniscule panes of glass. I shrank away from it.

"You know what this is, Jane? This is hair from the head of a woman struck by thunder three centuries ago. Now, we all know it's impossible to be struck by thunder. But not really, Jane, not really. It all depends on what we believe and how we say it. Now, Jane, you want to lose that wicked sister, don't you?"

"But why . . . how . . . can I bring you Tony's girl?"

I pulled the crucifix from the chain, wrenched it from my bosom and broke it in two. Why had Stephen given me this? A man handing a woman the effigy of a tiny man on a cross! I felt my fear recede once more. And Meg's demanding tone had changed and she was smiling. I noticed how familiar she suddenly seemed to me, as if in some way she was a part of myself, as if I had known her

for a long time. She reminded me of something, of myself
. . . of the figure in the clearing in the forest, who was
perhaps a part of herself for she had sent him . . . I felt
a balance return, as light and easy in that forbidding dark
red box as it had been in the even light and shade of the
forest ring. The snapped cross lay on the floor between us,
Christ's head and body at right angles to his feet.

"I'll show you how to bring her here." Meg was looking
down at me through eyes as slanting, mocking and clear
as those of the elusive figure in the fairy circle. I saw
suddenly that they were one and the same: if I brought
Meg what she desired he would indeed be mine. She had
only to conjure him from air, from leaves, from atoms,
from water and fire . . . Meg put her hands on my
shoulders and I felt him there. There was a violent lurch
in the pit of my stomach as my shadow struggled outside,
beating her head on the walls in an effort to get in and
take possession again.

"Who is he?" I said.

Meg's face was close to mine. Her eyes were shining.
Her lips parted. In the depths of her mouth the teeth were
as long and white and pointed as stalactites.

"Whatever you care to call him. He may be my brother,
he may be yours. Use the initial K for him, if you wish. A
bent line that comes in on a straight line and shoots it to
pieces! Or Gil-martin, that's my name."

From under the cherry red choker at Meg's neck two
drops of blood appeared. They stayed a moment defying
gravity on the stately white neck, then, leaving a tearful
trail of pale red, went down to the edge of her dress and

the white rose pinned there. The rose took the tinge. I stood fascinated. Meg was very pale now and her cheeks drawn, mouth open and wet and red behind the needles of white, upper lip arched as a rainbow. She pulled me to the corner, to the divan pushed up against a window—the divan covered with the white quilt and the scarlet diamonds of blood. She pushed me so that I fell backwards, and lay on the quilt, head butting the red velvet curtain that covered the window a few feet above my shadow's head.

"Jane!"

Meg's face had become huge above me. It blotted out the light, anonymous as the memory of a mother's face. From the sides of the vast head sprang her snake locks, and the rest of the room, the glass-topped tables with the strange relics from the days before science, the filing cabinets—God knows what she kept there: the names of her victims, the addresses of the invisible regions they would be permitted to visit?—lay beyond her without perspective. From the angle where I lay crushed, the objects and the dim red room seemed painted round her head, like detail in an icon, like stilted representations of figments of her imagination. As she leaned further over me, the redness became more interior . . . it was the redness of a bloodshot eye, it came from within me, particles of red spattered out in the dark room. I felt a total guilt . . . the weight of the guilt was Meg . . . I could do no right, I was the eternal victim. I floated in the horror of the guilt . . . but she pinned me down there . . . if she was going to kill me now, I wanted it. I was at one with her:

she was completely accusing, and I completely guilty.
And as I half-fainted, in the room which seemed en-
compassed behind the lids of my eyes, of red membrane
and buzzing dots of blood, I saw the witches Meg and I
had been: I saw us in the villages, in the mud streets,
hounded in the open country, with our charms, and old
hands with webbed fingers, and the gaze of self-righteous
accusation straight into our eyes like stakes. I felt the
hatred. I felt to blame. And yet . . . somewhere beyond
that . . . we had been happy together, in another country.
We had been whole.

"Jane! Open your eyes and look at me now!"

I did. I began to struggle, but I soon stopped. Meg's
white bosom lay over mine. In her throat the wounds
shone like a ferret's eyes. Beneath us, my sister beat her
head—slower and slower, like a collapsing heart—against
the door of Meg's house. I could feel he was somewhere
in the room, for Meg lay very still and as mine opened,
her eyes closed. Somewhere, over by the door to the red
landing, or in the far corner by the dark cupboard, he was
standing. He was made of red light, and dancing particles
of dust, and all the magic relics, amulets and cabbalistic
papers of Meg's collection. He had come as suddenly as a
flame when two sticks are rubbed together, and he was as
suddenly gone. But I felt his warmth, at the side of Meg's
cold white body.

The pain—ice splinters of pain for a second so intense
that I thought I heard my own scream, but there was no
scream, for it was there that the pain came, at the side of
my throat, and my larynx closed—threw my sister outside

onto the ground, and there was a thumping, and then silence. Meg's eyes were shut. Her teeth were still extended: her canines, her eye teeth which took blood and gave sight, jutted over her lower lip—my blood was on her chin and on the quilt, where it ran down into the scarlet lozenges as if they had been sewn in there for that purpose. Her face looked smaller again, a normal size: as she drank, perhaps, she bloated, or she needed that vastness to stun her prey. Her hair, free from the blood, lay in damp coils over the side of the bed. She was like a woman who has given birth, where there is exhaustion, and blood and sweat. Her breath was noisy, and fast.

I lay in a limbo. My sister was dead. My guilt was gone. I was as empty as if a hand had gone inside me and pulled out my guts. I had felt his presence, and Meg would bring him again. I felt such gratitude to her that I lifted my arm, which was as heavy as lead, and stroked the dark hair that hung over the side of the bed.

"Jane!" Meg's eyes opened.

"I'll do anything for you."

I was sure I had never said those words in my life. And as I said them, I knew she would make sure I still had my side of the bargain to fulfil. But she had given me the means to do it! I would bring such power to Meg, that she would be like a great Buddha on my blood.

Meg was smiling up at me. Her lips were together now, a faint red, bow-shaped.

"So you will bring me the girl?"

"Yes I will," I said.

TONY'S MOTHER WAS sitting in the flat, on the sofa where Tony and I sit as far apart as Martians and watch TV. She was doing several things, all of them characteristic: she was smoking, and waving her second and third fingers up and down with the cigarette between them, as if to admire her painted nails; with her other hand she was opening and shutting her bag—click!—and taking out her compact, which was white and frosted over with a goldish sheen; she was flicking open the compact lid with her thumb and raising the round mirror to her face, and making a strange little moue into it, as if she was trying to shrink her face down to fit the lid; and with her foot, in a pointed and high-heeled shoe, she was tapping to some fast and silent rhythm on the floor. I stood for a while and watched her from the doorway, but she knew I was there for she must have heard the front door slam, and I knew she knew she was putting on a performance to prove that Tony could give her the key of the flat whenever he liked. I wondered if she had put her overnight bag in the spare room without even asking me. It was probable. What terrible event had she come up from the country for this time? A 'delicious play', perhaps—but plays were getting too rough these days for Mrs Marten's delicate tastes. "As long as it's funnee," she would say with a sigh. "All I want is something fun-nee." She had walked out of nudity and agitprop, bewildered but still dignified, all the way to the Savoy. Or a 'dinner': perhaps there was a ball gown in my spare room now, bulging like an uninvited guest against the back of the door. The 'dinners' were in flats in Eaton Square, and there were hired footmen and gold chairs, vases of sweetpeas and lilies which were described afterwards with an odd laugh, as if they were in some way more significant to her than the people. She had seldom dared to stay more than one night. But now, with Tony away, I had the feeling she had come for longer. There was a bravado to the small shoulders in the perfectly cut coat. The chignon of flaxen white hair nodded, as the foot tapped and the little made-up face, hardly bigger than a gibbon's, stared at itself, rapt, on a far journey but still perfectly conscious of me there. Her hair was like the wool on the distaff of the wicked old woman who puts a castle to sleep for a hundred years—her whole person was the spindle, which pricks you through and through. I went towards her warily: I was tired and all I wanted to do then was to sleep, and after to speak to Gala. Her sharp, miniscule frame swung at the sound of my step and the curves of her lips followed the smile which was already painted on.

"There was no-one at the Bartons. Do you know Lady Lucy Barton? Oh. So I came on here. There's a 'do' this evening, Jane, at the Belgian Embassy. Do come!"

No sign of apology or explanation for being in my flat,

I noted. I gave her a stiff nod, no smile. Mrs Marten
seemed further away than ever now. Her cosmetics, her
concealed terrors of death or solitude were as poignant
and distant as the rigidified body of an unknown woman
preserved in lava. Her lifespan seemed tiny, concomitant
with her body: a butterfly span, a scarf. I felt I could see
her flutterings, her crumbling to chalk. She was smiling
still in my direction, eyes glinting from a bed of green
mascara and imitation lash.

"Jane dear, would it be awful to ask for a G and T?"

Oh God, I thought, Gala, where are you? Meg, come
soon and make a spell over this ghastly woman. But I
went to the drink cupboard at the other end of the sitting
room and took out the gin and tonic. Without asking, I
went to the kitchen for ice, and found half a mouldy old
lemon. Mrs Marten wanted her drinks with 'all the
trimmings', as if they weren't alcohol but instead some
sort of gay, childish drink, harmless and refreshing. I
scraped off the grey-green mould and put a slice of lemon
in the glass.

"How heavenly! Then I simply must have a bath. I do
hope my dress hasn't got too crumply! Well, Jane dear,
tell me all your news! Lots of exciting things been
happening?"

I smiled. I sat down on the armchair next to the sofa.
Perhaps I should tell her I was going all out to 'get'
Tony's girl—or the girl who had once been 'his', at least.
If I confided in Mrs Marten, would she suddenly tell me
something I didn't know: that Tony was indeed still
seeing the girl, for instance. Would she break his web of

lies, if he was in fact at the centre of one? No, of course she wouldn't. She would protect Tony for all she was worth. From that frail, expensively suited chrysalis Tony had come: his head had appeared between her legs to stare anxiously at the reversed order of things. She would guard him against 'predatory' ladies like me; she would have preferred me, but for my useful ownership of the flat, to have been an out-and-out victim. But little did she guess quite how predatory I had become! So I smiled again.

"Busy seeing films all the time? I really don't know how you do it! I find they've become so dreary, recently."

Privately I rather agreed with Mrs Marten, but I decided against saying so. The slightest mark of encouragement and she would move into the flat for the entire 'season'. As it was I was prepared to let her stay one night, then she could find friends, or go back to her home in the hills of Surrey where the woods and belts of trees looked like curtains on a swish rail, pulled across the sinister, semi-rural countryside.

"Yes, I've been seeing quite a few. Nothing I could recommend to *you*, I'm afraid."

After this blatantly snobbish remark on my part, we fell silent. The evening was beginning to come in the windows, there was the sound of the soft drinks crates being thumped down on the pavement outside Paradise Island. The parrot gave a squawk or two to greet the pale, untropical evening and Mrs Marten rolled the ice in her glass and tapped her foot and grinned like a skull in front of the blank TV. I reached for the evening paper she had

brought with her, to see what programmes were on later
—I might not sleep. I might watch instead. And I felt the
faint dampness on my legs, from the plants outside the
main entrance to the flat, the residue of rain showers and
the cuckoo spit which collected there. I brushed my leg
dry with the back of my hand, while Mrs Marten looked
with surreptitious horror at the lack of stockings or
tights. If only she could know how far I had been! Yet
for her, to go outside bare-legged would be an unimaginable step into the unknown.

While I was thinking these thoughts—tired, increas-
ingly irritated with her presence—the telephone rang.
Mrs Marten was on her feet before I could move. What
was this? Had she left the number here already to a host
of social secretaries? Were we to be *poste restante* for
summer invitations? It was because of Mrs Marten that
Tony and I had gone to the Berring party—she was a
'close personal friend' of the Berrings, and Tony, pretending enthusiasm, had insisted we go (who had
summoned Meg there? Had she simply followed me?).
Were we now to be subjected to more of this? I decided
to tell her, as soon as she was off the phone, that she must
leave by tomorrow morning. Friends were coming to
stay. And I thought—what a good idea—Gala could
come and keep me company, and help me in case I became
afraid thinking of Meg.

Mrs Marten was speaking low and fast into the
receiver. She presented her back to me as she did so, as
trim as an airport doll with its topping of nylon hair. Her
left hand waved a perpendicular cigarette and the scarlet

nails danced about like fish in an aquarium. "Yes. My dear, I wasn't sure . . . Yes . . . Yes. Look, Miranda, why not wait . . . no, not for two days more I think . . . Yes. Yes. I quite agree. But this is the trouble, Miranda . . ."

I felt a slow coldness, first in my stomach, but there was a wriggling and a fainting in my stomach too as if it had become a sack of fish, packed and anaesthetised by ice. Nerves jingled in my fingers and toes. Miranda. Of course, that was her name. It would be Miranda. She was smiling out at me from the photo in the kitchen drawer. At night she pursued me on my journeys, and chained me when I was about to escape. She stood under my window. . . . Meg had stunned her, but only for a while. . . . She was on the 'phone now to Tony's mother. And who better? The woman who must for every psychological reason detest me more than any other human being, was conniving with the other woman enemy. These two women—one who had carried Tony as a water creature, a nail-less monster, a blind, puckered parcel of flesh attached by a crusty yellow cord to her bag of food, who had finally pushed out into the world a man responsible for her future comforts, her Surrey home, her electric blanket and holidays abroad, and the other with whom, having crawled from between the legs of his mother, he had finally found refuge, plunging in again between her legs for safety—formed a wall against me, a society for my end. They would drive me mad, extinguish me, remove me. I had no place in Tony's unbearable trinity. And yet they wouldn't get away with it as easily as that! I gritted my teeth as Mrs Marten spoke, and thought of Meg. She was right in saying I could only do good by bringing the girl to her—that I would purify women's legion souls.

"Yes, dear, well why don't you come? Of course they won't mind. It's a buffet . . . but I'll tell them and I know they'll be thrilled. It's the Belgian Embassy, at eight. Well I'm wearing long, but at your age . . . lovely, dear. Goodbye."

Mrs Marten rang off. She turned in my direction with what was, I thought, a guilty smile. But no—as she came nearer she seemed actually triumphant. Her face looked even smaller, like a shrunken African head painted white.

"Who was that?" I said. I heard myself sound blunt, manly: somehow between them the mother and the true love had excluded me from their sex.

"Oh Jane darling, I don't think you know her. I'm so pleased to have someone to take to the Belgian Embassy party . . . I was simply dreading it alone . . ."

"Is she a friend of Tony's?"

"Well I suppose she *knows* him. As a matter of fact I think she's in the film world a tiny bit. She said something about the film . . . is it one of the books by that marvellous Joseph Conrad?"

"*Chance*," I said.

The phone rang again. This time, while Mrs Marten still stood in a mock-abject attitude before me, I rose to my feet, almost pushed her out of the way, and went over to answer it. Thank God, Gala's voice was loud and clear, strangely grating as it always was when she had been on her own for a time. She had guessed, of course. "Are you all right, Jane?" Gala said. "I was worrying about you. Where did you go today?"

"Come over," I said. "Can you?"

"Yes, but not for very long. I will though. I'll see you."

"Good," I said.

It was my turn now to face Mrs Marten from the other end of the sitting room. She was still directing at me her primitive-mask smile, her small eyes shone from the thick white pancake.

"You were asking about Miranda. Rather fascinating . . . it's an old theatrical family of course. No . . . she said just now they were going to ask Janet *Suzman* to be the heroine in the movie . . . Isn't that rather exciting? I don't know how she knew of course . . ."

No I bet you don't. She's been with Tony, or she's been speaking to him. I nodded at Mrs Marten as if I had received important news on the telephone and failed to sit down, which left us standing awkwardly, like people at one of the cocktail parties Mrs Marten loved so much.

"Janet Suzman as Flora de Barral," I said. "Yes, that sounds very interesting." Inside me, at last, a great wave of laughter was coming, and with it the strength to abolish the woman who brought me so much pain, who stood in my way. (Gala was coming. She would help me.) "I'm afraid I have a friend coming to stay tonight unexpectedly," I said. "Her husband has just died. So I can't invite you to stay after all!"

I had never behaved like this before. I saw Mrs Marten step back from me as if I had just announced a leprous condition, then, with infinite care, she approached me

143

again and put her arms on my shoulders. Her eyes in the buried face looked up at me with a passable but exaggerated show of sympathy.

"Jane, do you know you're looking a little pale today? I'm feeling ever so slightly worried about going out and leaving you here. And I couldn't help noticing, when your scarf slipped . . . you seem to have hurt your throat. Is there anything poor old Mother can do?"

"I'm sorry. This is really the situation." I could hear the firm gruffness of my voice, I could see Mrs Marten's ball dress being bundled into a suitcase and away to a cheap hotel, I could feel Mrs Marten's terror. "There won't be time for a bath, or time to change, I'm afraid," I said. "She's coming now, you see, and she needs every care."

Why was it that it appeared more cruel to treat a woman like Mrs Marten in that way than to do far worse to a person really in need of care? She was so outraged. The monkey face began to gibber. I took her stick arm, with a sense of revulsion, and led her through the hall to the spare room where she had made herself at home.

"Now pack," I said.

"Well, Jane, I don't know what Tony will say!" Mrs Marten stood in the centre of the room, arms akimbo, like an expensive scarecrow. "You aren't well, Jane, I fear!"

"I'll call a mini-cab," I said.

Five minutes later, Mrs Marten and the ball dress, which lay in a polythene bag like a slumped body, and the suitcase, and even the smell of her scent that made me think always of the chintz armchairs in her Surrey house and the sickly roses that grew outside, had left the flat. I went to the sitting room to wait for Gala. I was weak, and my heart was pounding. I prayed she wouldn't be long.

Waiting is painful because it is an eternal present. The past is frozen, the future atrophied. And objects become lifeless too: the armchair which a short time ago contained Mrs Marten, had been an indispensable part of her maddening pose, is square and stiff as a chair in a hyper-realist painting. The cloth on the round table goes down to the ground in folds that could never be disturbed. On the table are a half-dead geranium in a pot, a tubular straw container which was made to put a glass in, in a tropical country where sweat and heat make glasses drop from hands—it holds broken fibre tip pens, and out-of-date postage stamps—and a pile of books and papers, all covered with a fine film of invisible, immoveable dust. I sit like an object myself, one leg crossed over the other—it would be as hard to part them as to roll two tree trunks in opposite directions. My left arm is firmly down on the arm rest of the settee. My right hand holds a glass of white wine, which is from time to time raised to my mouth. In this state of permanent suspension, I wait.

Night has come down on the street now that Tony's mother has gone. But I am distant from it, hanging in a cage of light above dark pavements and the slow tread of battered wives who go out in threes for safety, and the beginning of the pounding hum from Paradise Island. I am a rectangle of yellow light, and tonight there is no round moon sailing in on me. I am empty and square as a windowpane. Only my throat aches. What will Gala say to that? And what will happen now? As the room shows no sign that Gala will ever come, I can think of no answers. The only objects that seem to move in my mind are the clothes I wore for my first journey—the jeans and narrow-shouldered jacket still, I suppose, in the washbasket in the kitchen. I can see them more clearly than the things round me in this room yet it may be I will never put them on again. How can I 'bring' this girl to Meg? How can I do it? She will have me stuck here like a fly if I don't move.

The thought only paralyses me further. I see Tony and Miranda together in a car, they are travelling fast through rain while I am glued here, they are smiling at each other like people in a film and there is the red glow of a cigarette level with her face. They are talking but I can't hear them. There are such big rainspots on the window that her face seems to have run a little, to have grown lopsided: but she is still beautiful. She is an enigma, she is deep. I am shallow, one white plane.

I see Meg. We are at the limit of a wood and beyond that is ice which is very crisp under the moon. We climb onto a sledge. We go fast over the ice. We are at war—we are chasing or being chased—but the ice wind is so cold that my face is frozen and I can't hear what Meg is calling to me. When the trees disappear, I am in terror: there is only the expanse of white ice as far as the eye can see. If it could crack, even! But it won't. There will be no black, ice-cold, welcoming gush. Just the ice, and us going fast over it like witches in our sledge.

I try to see him again. Of course this is impossible. He is the void. Meg won't show him again until I bring her what she wants. I am frozen because he isn't here. The lack of him has chained the objects in this room to their places, and has stopped the clocks so Gala will never come, and has filled the world with somnambulists who turned the world upside down, walking themselves one-eyed, Cyclopean, seeing from the eye in the ass the mess they made of it all. When it's night they say it's day. I sit in this artificial day without him—not even able to make the expected clucking noises, not able to produce what I'm expected to produce. Soon they'll get rid of me perhaps—sterile, expendable. But what could I have done to please them anyway? Strut for a few years, push out unwanted babies, find part-time 'fulfilment', take the blows or the eternity ring, die?

From under the table with the telephone a bright green triangular edge of cardboard—a part of Tony's address book—is sticking out on the carpet. A blob of Mrs Marten's cigarette ash lies on it, and it's because the colour of the book so resembles the colour of the ash that I start forward in my seat and then freeze again, this time with my arms out in front of me in the air. I had only imagined that bright green—in reality it's grey to me! So—it's happened already. And I almost feel relief. Until Meg frees me . . . yet the thought is too horrible and I turn away from it. Deuter Jane, who can see no green in the real world, who must leave the world to breathe. My palms, which are still stretched out and a foot apart from each other as if I were about to clap, begin to run with sweat. I am the bad throw of the dice. I am the double, now it's me who's become the shadow. Where I was haunted, now I will pursue. And the world will try to stamp me out, as I run like a grey replica of my vanished self—evil, unwanted, voracious in my needs. I will be outcast, dogging the steps of stronger women, fastening myself onto them at nights, trailing as their lying shadow in the day. Unless . . . bringing the world to rights . . . bringing to Meg's red altar the essential sacrifice . . . I am restored to life and greenness and in tearing out the simulacrum need no longer live as one myself. I can feel my legs tense as I prepare for the journey across the room to that triangle of grey board. My hands go down on the settee and give a push . . . slowly, deliberately, I go through the ever-greying room.

I never knew Tony knew so many people. A lot of them seem to have moved several times since he first inscribed their names, there are crossings-out and rehousings on every page. What does he do with these people? There is something ridiculous about the address book—it makes me laugh to think of Tony's serious face as he copies them out. Does he 'go through' the book to discover whom he feels like seeing? It's true we gave a party once, and he used the book with an air of triumph, but the party wasn't much of a success. Nobody seemed to know what they were doing there: perhaps they felt they had walked straight out of Tony's address book and couldn't wait to get back in there again.

My hands are clumsy and the pages turn over in clumps

as I look for her. M . . . why should she be in under her
first name anyway? But I have a feeling she is. M for
mother, for murder, for Meg. M for her. She made me a
shadow, discarded by Tony before he had even met me.
I am in Meg now, for Meg has my blood, and soon, M,
you will be. We'll both be there. Together again! But this
time I'll be the strong one, you'll see.

Monica . . . the name in faded pencil and no surname
. . . I smile in spite of myself at the idea that Tony went to
prostitutes. But how can you tell anything about people?
I see Monica in a flat in a redbrick mansion in Chelsea,
opening the door in a clinging black sweater and tossing
her head. Tony makes a foolish face. They go in and the
door closes behind them. No. Monica, it's not you.
Margaret . . . Margaret has changed her name and address
so many times that her different married names pile up to
the right of her like the corpses of flies—in the end Tony
must have decided she was simply Margaret. Oh,
Margaret, why did you marry so often? Did you believe
there was going to be happiness and content? Didn't you
see the world in grey sometimes, didn't someone come
and take your substance away? How optimistic you must
have been, every time you left the Registry office and
went off to buy a new casserole, material for comforting
curtains that would screen you and your new mate off
from the outside world! Did you tire of them quickly . . .
or did you kill them perhaps, like Bluebeard, and leave
them in a small room with their congealed blood? For
you must be quite rich, Margaret, you live in an expensive
area. Did they marry you for your money and your

casseroles and then play a double game? They two-timed you, there seems little doubt about that.

Miranda . . .

Now I've found her I don't know what to do. I was right, Tony had simply put in the first name, for him she has no second name unless it's his. She is a part of him. She lies right on the middle of the page in the middle of the book. M the thirteenth letter, the centre of the alphabet, the centre of his world. She is written in a careful sloping hand, as if every letter was stroked as it went down, and she is in a strong black ink he doesn't seem to use otherwise except for the addresses of solicitors and doctors. This makes her official somehow, and obedient to him—for although the ink is strong the curve of the letters is feminine and submissive. Maybe she wrote her name herself? But there is something of Tony in the writing: together they entered her in his life.

Miranda lives at 114 Albert Drive, the other side of the river. Albert Bridge which is strung with coloured lights at night—on a dark night they make a red and yellow and green road above the bridge—leads to Miranda. I can see Tony walking the aerial road, arms outstretched in the artificial faery glow . . . dropping down into the blackness to take her in his arms. But this time, Miranda, it's me that's coming to see you. I'll go over the water and I'll bring you back. And I almost laugh, squatting there on the grey carpet by the grey TV screen, with Mrs Marten's cigarette ash scattered on the floor. This is Caliban calling, Miranda . . . When I've delivered you where you belong, I'll be myself again.

At first I misdial the number. My fingers are numb, and for some reason I don't feel like sitting down properly, so I stay in squatting position and it makes me unbalanced and shaky in my arms and legs. Then finally I get it right. As it rings I stare across the room at the window . . . ah, I'd like to fly out there now and not make this call. Or . . . why didn't I close the curtains? Suppose there's a wave of laughter and singing from Paradise Island or a fracas in the wives' home at the appearance of a drunken husband —I won't be able to hear what Miranda has to say.

In fact, a silence seems to fall on the street as Miranda answers. There are no footsteps, the parrot no longer fills the puncture it has pierced in the air, the clink and thwack of the Schweppes bottles has entirely stopped. I can hear Miranda breathing as if her throat were two inches from mine.

"Is that Miranda?"

"Yes?"

"This is Jane."

In Miranda's silence, the street begins to come to life. Right under my window, from where she used to stand, a man gives one of those shouts that are meant to communicate nothing, that are just a man's shout, like a dog's bark. But the shout hangs in the street: in response a wooden crate drops and a window goes up with an ear-splitting yawn.

"What do you want?"

"I thought . . . I thought you'd gone out this evening with . . . with Mrs Marten. You didn't?"

"What? With whom?"

"To some embassy . . ."

"What Jane *is* this?"

Now that's a good question! You know very well, Miranda—but perhaps you're not being so disingenuous after all. Have you also dreamed of me? Do you know you follow me wherever I go?

"With Tony's mother," I say. "I'm sorry, it must have been another Miranda."

A pause. Miranda is thinking. I can feel her think and I can see two blue veins in her throat, pulsing.

"Yes I did go actually," she says. "Earlier."

My first thought is prosaic. Whatever time can it be now? How long did I sit waiting for Gala? Then I freeze. The bitch! How cool and collected she sounds! What on earth is she doing with Tony's mother? I refuse to accept that she must have had a relationship with Tony's mother long before I met Tony. Tony, after all, only existed for me when I met him—Miranda too through him. It has always been impossible to imagine Miranda sitting in Mrs Marten's home in the Surrey hills, flipping through magazines and making plans, quite unaware of my being in the world.

"I think I'd better ring off," says Miranda.

She thinks I'm drunk, hysterical. She knows, from what Tony has told her, that he can't wait to leave me and be with her again.

"Miranda! I'm only ringing to ask you to a party. As we've never met . . . it seems so silly really . . ."

"A party?" Miranda sounds suspicious. Tony has probably told her by now, on the phone from Rome airport or a Geneva hotel where he lies groaning for her at night, of my obsession with her photo. So why am I asking her to a party? But I'm good at this. I didn't get my job for nothing.

"I just think you'd enjoy it. And it seems a bit ridiculous that we can't ever meet . . . as if Tony was standing between us like the sword of Damocles! No . . . it's a party the day after tomorrow at Miles Alton's house . . . yes the man who makes . . . exactly . . . And as I know you're doing sets at the moment for that film . . ."

"Where is it?"

Miranda's voice is still very cool but I can hear the excitement, buried under layers of ice. How clever of me to remember that Miles Alton's party is in fact the day after tomorrow . . . is that Thursday . . . yes it is . . . and consciously I haven't given the matter a thought since the card came weeks ago. Of course she'll want to meet him, he's one of the few good film directors. Of course she'll want to be asked to design his next film. Can't she just see herself doing it—in Hollywood with any luck—she'll wear black, with a V neck. I can't help smiling at my vulgar jealousy. But I know I've caught her, fair and square.

"14 Sloane Gardens," I say. "All one house, one bell. About eight onwards."

"I'll see if I can make it. Well thank you, Jane, for asking me."

We say goodbye and ring off. For a long time I stay crouched on the floor. Two more days, before Tony comes back . . . before the party . . . before seeing Meg again.

We were in my bedroom, Gala and I. Where Tony lies, on the side of the bed nearest the window, his shoulders hunched and his back to me as if in a state of perpetual shrug, Gala sat and smoked, her spine up against the wall. She was late because her sculptor had come to see her—they'd gone out to supper then he'd had to go back to the country again—and her eyes were bright, her movements sudden. She had embarked on an evening with him, and I felt that only a part of her was with me. I lay diagonally from her on the end of the bed, with the big square ashtray between us. Her legs swayed as she spoke, in a secret dance, and her arms swooped and circled. Her energy crept into me, through my veil of tiredness and confusion.

"Were you afraid then, Jane?"

"Yes. Yes I was. I can't believe that's what she wants me to do."

"Oh I think you do believe it. You do believe it's right."

Yes. Gala, as always, could recognise a past feeling spoken in the present, smell its wrongness. I did now believe Meg. But why? How? I was in two worlds, and slipping into the abyss between them. My actions showed my growing belief. My spoken thoughts were firmly in the world I lived in with Tony, and work, and that muddle of hope and defeat which everyone drags with them through the day. But if I were really to go after Miranda . . .

"You realise you were very lucky to be chosen," Gala said. "She must see the potential in you, Jane. There are only a very few people like you, you know. . . . Don't you think you *are* fortunate, Jane, to be one of us?"

I stared at Gala, who was more animated than ever now. She seemed to be speaking to someone else as well as to me; her eyes were fixed on the wall opposite and in her persuasiveness I almost felt the street move and stand to attention beneath her. With her will she was pulling the world into her hands. . . . But the bump of rock music from Paradise Island went on, and a car stopped with a screech at the pedestrian crossing outside the super-market with the cardboard dolls.

"But, Gala, do you know the answers?"

"Where do you think my sculpture comes from, Jane? It can make no difference yet, but Meg has sent me on journeys where I can gather it up. She's shown me the way. I can't do what you can do, though—I can't bring Meg what she needs for the next stage. Come on, Jane, you've given her your blood. Now bring her that shadow to destroy!"

The hair of the head of a woman struck by thunder. I could see it, coiled between the glass slides, terrifying symbol of Meg's power. I felt weak—my body was numb —only Gala's current kept me conscious. I found myself nodding though the rebellion was in me still like a small fish struggling to swim upstream.

"Why should it be me, Gala? Surely . . ."

"Perhaps it corresponds with your external situation," Gala said briskly. I knew she was uninterested in my life with Tony, in my exasperations and jealousies. In fact, she seemed to have little belief in my external life at all. She and Meg together had translated me into this new zone and for them it was my sole existence. Was I to be their guinea pig, going from the known to the unknown and changed at their will?

"You remember how you felt about the first trip Meg sent you on," Gala said. "Don't you want to travel again?"

Ah, of course I did! The walls of the room where we sat were straining to be rid of me. Down the corridor, long and winding and grey in the eye of my exhaustion, there lay the kitchen and the washbox and the small, battered clothes and the door out onto the fire escape and the void. And all I had to do . . .

"We'll be proud of you," Gala said. "Jane, you look very pale. Are you all right?"

"I'm a bit drained," I said, and we both laughed. "No, I think I'd better get into bed. Don't worry, Gala, I've already made the first moves for what Meg wants."

"Have you? Have you really?" Gala leaned across the bed and gave me a sharp stare. "Ah!"

"Tell me about K, though, or Gil-martin—I don't understand."

"You will!" Gala motioned to me to get under the covers. "I'll bring you some tea now. Jane, he can only be insubstantial at present, for you haven't rid yourself of your double female self yet. You could call him the male principle, which you lack . . . or . . ."

"Yes," I said. "All right, Gala. All right. I'll wait. I'll go to sleep now."

I lay under the covers, and listened to Gala taking cups out of the cupboard in the kitchen. She came with the tea, and biscuits that had gone soft with age. I ate and drank, although I hardly had the strength to lift my hand. When we had finished, Gala brought the TV in from the sitting room and we watched the last hour—Richard Nixon, as he explained away his past.

Gala was smiling, my eyes were half-shut but I could feel her pleasure and excitement.

"You see, Jane! No-one could believe his language, the language of Watergate! It remains to us to lose our evil selves and speak again!"

Through my lowered eyelids I stared at Nixon's face. It may have been the effect of a reddish blur from the inner lids themselves, or it may have been my imagination, but his grey face seemed every moment to become more pink. A roseate blur surrounded the set, and slowly filled the room. I closed my eyes altogether, into a red nothingness.

"Everything looked so grey earlier," I mumbled to Gala. "And now it's turning red. As for green, I can't see it at all."

"We all have that," Gala said. "We must suffer it until the day comes, as you say. And you must rest, Jane, as you're the one who will bring it about!"

I slept then. Gala stayed the night in the spare room, where Mrs Marten had tried to introduce her ball gown. She said she would come to me early in the morning, with more tea and a boiled egg. I must rest. She advised me to rest as much as I could. I must be healthy, and there was a great deal of preparation ahead.

I WOKE THE next morning feeling extraordinarily well
and happy, as if I had been purged of all the miseries of
the grey street outside, and the grey shadow that used to
live inside me, knocking against my ribs in her effort to
get out, and the weight of my own double face in public
places. I was bled of it all. I was free. I knew I must re-
visit the old haunts again, that Meg would make me do
this so that I could settle my scores with my sisters there
before settling once and for all in this world with Miranda, but I no longer felt any doubt of my future . . . the
journeys . . . K or Gil-martin: they were all mine and I
would leave on my ship soon to enjoy them. I felt even
frivolous: memories of Tony's mother—another Mrs
Marten, but how different from Meg!—made me smile as
I lay in bed waiting for Gala. Poor Mrs Marten! Had she
had a good time at her Embassy dance? How could she
know, setting off to meet her dear Miranda, that it was
the last time they would go out together? But, when you
added up what there was in it for Mrs Marten, would she
really care? She would lose a daughter and gain a son—
no, she would lose two daughters, for no doubt she saw
me as a daughter too, an unwelcome one—and yet, when

her grief for Miranda was over, she would after all have Tony for herself. She would imprison him in Surrey while he wept for Miranda and told her again and again that he couldn't understand how I could have brought myself to do it. She would marry him, fill his fat, disconsolate body with suet and lumps of meat and potatoes, sew his feet into his socks, sometimes take him out to look at the autumn trees that were so disconcertingly like curtains. He would play bridge, and give up his film career. Or would he go on with the script of *Chance*, year in, year out, playing with the concept of two narrators, two male 'voices over' discussing the pride and shame of poor Flora de Barral. I would be a long way away by then, of course. I, who had recounted my own life and taken my own decisions rather than have them recounted or taken for me, would he think of me sometimes, in his chintzy eunuch's bedroom, as I sailed the high seas? I doubted it. Mrs Marten would put an opiate in the tea from Jackson's. I would be blocked from his mind for good.

These enjoyable fantasies were broken by Gala's appearance in my room with a messily made up breakfast tray, a cracked egg and a slice of burnt toast. She had made coffee instead of the promised tea, and the smell was strengthening: I realised that however well I might feel I was still very weak. I thanked Gala and took the coffee with a shaky hand.

"Did you sleep all right, Jane? How are the colour problems?"

"Still a little rosy!" I smiled up at her—Gala seemed

very grey still, while the rest of the room was bathed in the red spots Meg had bequeathed, like the dots in a comic. I raised myself to look out of the window—sure enough, the tops of the sparsely leaved plane trees in the street had lost their dull, London green. A slight wind shook them, and they danced like spirals of smoke against the grey houses. It came to me that in my memories of Mrs Marten in Surrey, the colours had all been normal. And despite my happiness I felt the shudder of the premonition of death. Where I walked, the colour of life was drained away. There was life only in my memories. I was already the walking dead, a shadow, drawn to my old life in search of the green.

"Don't worry," Gala said. "You're between regions, Jane. You're about to embark. Now eat your egg! I'm sorry it cracked, but it's a battery egg, it must be. Thank your lucky stars you weren't born a battery hen, my dear!"

I laughed, and felt some of the new frivolity return. If my new powers were beginning, what tricks I could play on the world before I finally bowed out! If my words became truth, I could literally destroy the film I disliked or disapproved of: under my acid gaze the celluloid would turn to muddy water and run away. How I could tease poor Stephen, by substantiating his Christ on the cross for him, right in his sitting room as he handed out his sweet cakes to young men with burning cheeks! How it would torment him . . . what would he do? Go down on his knees by the bleeding feet . . . seize the dark emaciated legs? I laughed aloud. And Tony, I could set him dancing with Miranda and make sure they never could stop. I would hire them out on a cruise ship to South America, as dancing lovers, allowed only to pause for a few moments and refresh themselves with champagne. I would call the tune faster and faster, until Tony fell on his back and was pushed to the side in ignominy, and Miranda . . . ah, Miranda . . . I would call Taranta! . . . and what could she do but obey me, she the woman in a sexual, hysterical frenzy, the spider-bitten woman trembling and shaking in the poison of her wants. There! She tries to slow but she can't: in *her* marathon there'll be no dragging steps.

"Jane!"

Through the open door of my bedroom I saw Gala's legs coming from the kitchen. I was disappointed, I felt moist with excitement at Miranda's humiliation, I saw for a moment the posters in the Underground where I had passed, every day as a woman child, the alluring figures of other women, whom I must become or emulate but was forbidden to love. I felt the bitter sting of my own defeat then, when I had first felt the other woman stir in my breast and point to the beautiful and impossible breasts of others. I saw the eyes of the crowd on Miranda, as her silk dress was ripped from her and she danced naked, screaming with pain. There was laughter on the ship, as the rich men savoured the sight. And I had tried to be the woman of the posters and yet not to love her . . . to be myself and her, and to please the world. My hands slid between my legs: I waited upright for Gala to reach my room.

"It's bad news, I'm afraid." Then Gala saw my expression. "Now, Jane, only two more days to go before you're whole again! Wait. He's waiting for *you*. But in the meantime, I have to tell you the unfortunate news that Tony is back. And his mother seems to be with him. They're coming in the main gate at the moment. D'you want me to go? I could use the fire escape in the kitchen, couldn't I?"

Dear Gala! I jumped out of bed, kicked the door of my room shut behind her, and threw my arms round her thin body. Where would I be without Gala? Still going off with a sinking heart and a sense of duty to my job, still bored and jealous with Tony, still trapped in a greyness far worse than the actuality of the state of the world provided by Meg. I would have no prospect of becoming whole at all. And there I was, in my miserable state of the past, when I should have been preparing for the great deed of tomorrow night. How did I imagine I was going to bring it off, after all? Did I think it would be easy, to kidnap Miranda, who would have no desire whatever to go with me? And in front of two hundred people. I trembled with agitation, standing there in my nightdress and listening to the horrible clang of the main door and the scrape of suitcases on lino.

"Well . . . which do you want me to do?"

"Stay, Gala, for heaven's sake!" I clutched her arm. "I feel . . . I feel afraid."

Gala pushed me away and looked at me severely. "You don't seem very rested, Jane. What are the plans, then, before they come?"

"At the . . . at the party." I was stuttering: I could hear

Tony at the flat door with his key, and the shrill, self-consuming laugh of his mother.

"At Miles Alton's party . . ." Had I already told Gala or not? I felt confused, almost as if the party were already over and the deed done. As so often when there was about to be a confrontation with Tony, my colour went up, and my head throbbed; but this time it was worse, as if Mrs Marten's opiates had already been at work.

"Don't panic!" Gala hissed at me. "It only helps them. Now, can you make this party a fancy dress party, do you think?"

"A fancy dress party?" I thought Gala must have gone out of her mind, when there were more important things to do then prance about in borrowed clothes.

"Try!" Gala said. "Go on, think about it hard. Try!"

As Tony and Mrs Marten came up the haircord stairs and stood exchanging unnecessary remarks—they didn't know whether or not I was there and they wanted to test the atmosphere, to sense if I was lying in wait for them, hostile—Gala took hold of me roughly and pushed me into the corner of my room by the window. Struggling to be free of her, I pressed my head up against the pane: through the layer of dirt I saw the Persian students in the house opposite, with reflected sun from my windows striking their gold sunflower rooms. . . . A succession of old women on the pavement below going past as if on a conveyor belt, motionless and lumpy, carrying parcels. . . . Two women in jeans brushing up broken glass from the steps of Paradise Island and then standing back, hands on hips, to enjoy the sun. A lovely summer day! The first real day of summer! And it was sparkling crystal grey to me, while the light summer breeze tossed leaves and ruffled grass the colour of black and white film. I stared through the frame of the window, as if from a million miles away. Gala's grip was still tight on me. Tony and his mother went into the sitting room and sat down, still keeping up an artificially loud conversation.

"Just do what I say," Gala said. "You'll understand when the time comes!"

I closed my eyes, and reluctantly I thought of the party where the conflict would be resolved. First I saw Miles Alton, whom I hardly knew. He was taking ice from the icebox. His hair was long and golden. There were candles everywhere, and guests were coming up the stairs. I sighed at the banality of the vision. What on earth did Gala want? Perhaps to introduce Meg and Gilmartin, by way of disguise. My interest quickened. They would be there then, would they? We would carry the drooping body of Miranda together to Meg's house. K would come towards me with a smile I could almost see. So, in fancy dress . . . I closed my eyes harder, shutting out the movements of the street and the unbalanced, reddish room where I stood with Gala. I saw a man dressed as a monk, with a cowl pulled over his face. I saw a twist of full taffeta skirt as the stair was turned. I saw a face that had become detached from a face. . . .

"Jane!" Tony was rattling the doorknob, as if the door was locked. "Are you there? I'm back, you know!"

"Well?" said Gala softly. "What do you see, Jane?"

"The face has slanting eyes," I said. "It stands on a stick.

But there's no soul behind the eyes, Gala. What does that
mean?"

"Jane, why did you lock the door? I hear you're not
terribly well and I want to come in. Come on now, Jane!"

I turned to Gala, who still had me by the arm. I opened
my eyes. Irritation . . . the red-dotted room was the colour
of irritation . . . my vision was broken just as it began.

"Why did you lock the door, Jane? For God's sake
open it!"

Gala went to open the door. I sank on the bed. I felt at
a disadvantage, still in my nightdress with Tony there
coated with the dust of International Airports, and his
mother, who must have been up and covered in cosmetics for hours. I gazed down at my arms, which looked
thin and white. How could it be me who would save the
world, bring about conjunction when there had been so
great a fissure? I was no more than a fragment myself.
How many broken corners of humanity did Meg lure to
her web in this way?

"A most disappointing trip! Rome was far too hot!
And the worst bit of miscasting for years. Woody Allen
as Captain Anthony. Really!"

Tony was sitting on my bed. I had the unpleasant feeling he had been there for some time. He had a hand on
my leg and his hand was warm: the nylon nightdress was
beginning to sweat under his touch. I saw that Gala had
gone. There was the sound of voices from the next room.
What could Mrs Marten and Gala, inhabitants of universes
as remote from each other as the stars from the earth,
ever find to say to each other?

"But, Jane . . ." (For I still made no move: I knew I was 'acting catatonic' and there was nothing I could do about it) "I heard worrying reports from Mummy! Were you . . . did you really have to be so rude?"

This shifted me of course. I pushed Tony's hand away and stood up. Then I turned to face him, as if the bedroom had become some kind of tribunal. Tony's face was at least as red as Nixon's had been last night, I noticed. It was splotchy, as if the colour needed adjusting, and went into a vivid orange by his receding hairline. "Do you honestly believe that it's my duty to put your mother up whenever she feels like coming to London?" I said. We had had this row so often that I saw Tony's features relax into spectator folds. It was my part to play the Japanese Noh theatre, and his to sit and growl from a distance.

"But you might have been a little more polite," Tony mumbled.

"And so might she! She was just sitting here!"

"And where had you been?"

Ah, that's a good one! In the metal forest, my dear Tony, in Meg's white house with the red heart. In the forest clearing too, betraying you!

"I don't like the way she sees Miranda, and asks her to parties, and expects me not to mind!"

"Miranda?" Tony looked surprised. He glanced with a worried expression at the bedside table, to see if the photograph had been resuscitated there. We never normally call her by her name—that's why, too, he seemed particularly uncomfortable. I saw him wondering if I'd been to see Miranda: what I'd been 'up to' now.

"She's welcome to see Miranda, as long as she doesn't sponge off me," I went on unnecessarily. "Surely, Tony, you can see that?"

"But Miranda means nothing more to me . . . to her I mean . . . than an old friend . . . really, Jane. . . ."

"Please ask your mother to leave the flat!"

I wasn't to be allowed that, though. The bedroom door opened—just as Tony was coming towards me in an attempt to remonstrate and give a kiss at the same time—and Mrs Marten put her head round it. Her body, which was in a white summer two-piece and very high white shoes, followed.

"My dear Jane, how are you this morning? Tony, don't you think . . . Jane looks so terribly *pale*. I *do* think you ought to have a holiday, Jane dear! Tony—be gallant! Take Jane away somewhere for some air!"

I saw Tony looking at me in the way he always did when he had decided I was menstruating. This would account for my rude behaviour, and also my paleness: I had discovered, in fact, that it could account for anything and therefore removed any proper claim I had to identity, as pre, post or current bleeding was always at the root of the problem. The same thought clearly went through the mind of Mrs Marten, and mother and son carefully failed to exchange glances.

"If only I could get this film settled," said Tony, with the very definite air of a man who has no intention of going on holiday. "But then we will . . . Mummy . . . Jane!"

"Gala your friend was telling me about the party tomorrow," Mrs Marten went on. She crossed the room as if she had been invited to feel at ease there, and glanced out of the window. From where I stood I could see her profile in a buzzing orange that looked as if the colour overlay had been badly applied, and beneath her in the street a battered wife with her child making for the super-market and the tanned cut-out women guarding the goods. She stared at them, oblivious of their existence. I turned angrily to Tony, but he was unpacking a small bag on the end of the bed and pulling out a dressing gown.

"I love fancy dress parties," Mrs Marten said.

"Who said it was fancy dress?"

"Oh . . . I . . . I don't know. I just assumed it was. Did your friend tell me? I can't remember, darling. Why? Didn't you know? Haven't you got an outfit?"

Even Tony was beginning to be annoyed now, I was pleased to see. He clearly thought the best way to set me right again was to spend some time alone with me, and the presence of both Gala, whom he detested, and his mother, about whom he felt constantly guilty, was getting on his nerves.

"I want to have a bath," he snapped. "What is this party anyway? Do you mind, Mummy, I want to change and so on?"

"Dear, I'm so sorry and tactless!" Mrs Marten turned away from my view, having raped my private knowledge of the street from that angle, taking with her in the retina of her eye green trees and grass I couldn't see, and went girlishly to the door. "I'll chat to your friend again, Jane! So fascinating to talk to artists. I used to know dear

John Masefield, you know! But we'll all have a wonderful time at the masked ball, I'm sure of that!"

A masked ball. Of course, a masked ball. I saw the faces without eyes, floating in the dark rooms. Behind one of them was Meg . . . behind another was my dark, unknown enemy. The faces walked on sticks . . . I had to tear them from their owners' heads. I pulled the eyes through the holes in the white paper heads.

Tony had his arms round me. He always wanted to make love when he came back from these trips, as if it was the only thing that could ground him properly again. So he was concerned about my condition.

"Have you got the curse today?" he whispered. His tongue shot into my ear. I shrank from him, then pretended to succumb.

"No. But I've lost a lot of blood," I said.

Tony made a satisfied, clucking sound—I was OK, now, then. He pulled me over to the bed. I lay under him. It was true, I was weak from loss of blood. There were red spots in front of my eyes, and whiteness, like when you are about to faint. I thought of the ball. Behind a mask on a long stick, prowling the dimly lit rooms, was Gil-martin, his shadow falling over me and replacing mine.

Tony's eyes were closed as he did his thrusting. Mine were open, my head was to the side of him, and his mouth was fastened in a sucking shape a few inches above Meg's bites, of which he was as yet oblivious. I stared up at the ceiling at the naked light bulb. There had been a shade once, but the paper had cracked and it had fallen, and I had never bothered to replace it. The bulb swung slightly, from the draughts that always manage to penetrate the flat, even when the windows and doors are shut. It swung above me, on a brown flex. It swung back and forth, globular, growing in size, bursting from the ceiling like a giant droplet of dew. I saw faces there, and as Tony sawed into me I saw clouds in its full roundness, and the street in miniature upside down. Mrs Marten and Gala were talking next door—or at least Mrs Marten was talking to Gala, constructing an identity for herself, turning it around for the customer to see in the light, like a new mink coat. Tony drove on, powered like the planes which roar in and deposit him in different corners of the world. I divided for him, but my new emptiness made me slip away. I was no longer truly under him, a match of his own making. I was oblique, I was half-filled, I was diagonal. And as if he felt me disappear, he gripped all the harder until the bulb above me dissolved, and the faces and people spilled into the room.

It's strange, to lie to the side of Tony and slightly above him, and see my own body still in his clamp, I can feel that people are searching for me . . . but they don't look there. I don't care to look down on my face. Suppose it weren't my own! And part of me still holds the sheet, so it must be me. Am I naked? No, I seem to be in a skirt like a little girl's skirt, so where are my jeans and jacket, if I'm to leave now on another journey? I am floating almost up to the level of the light bulb—can the Persian students opposite see me, flying without a carpet? The thought makes me smile. Am I taking this light-headedness with me to the other world? And the shopping women, some of whom look up into the sky on their return from the supermarket—will it rain today, wouldn't it be good to put the washing out for once?—do they see my weight-less state under the swinging bulb?

In the crystal ball that hangs just beyond my reach I can see Meg in her red house, eating at her round table with a man. Below me in the room, Tony and my body are still locked, but there are other people there now, and a feeling of airlessness and suffocation as the room fills up. The red glow has disappeared, as if drawn back into the bulb, into the filaments of Meg and her companion. Above the crowd, which makes no sound at all, I swim fascinated a few inches from the bulb. Meg has a red and white spotted scarf on her head, like a gypsy scarf. Gil-martin—for I know it is him—is staring into the fire. In my peace and emptiness, I circle over him. He doesn't look up, but I have no need to see his face. We had rough times together when we were children, he and I! Then I lost him. He looks the same, a little sadder perhaps. For his sake I'll bring the shadow woman Meg needs, I'll drag her like a dead vole to their front door.

Meg is saying something. K leans towards her to listen. Both their faces are distorted in the rotundity of the light bulb, like funfair faces. I can see myself in him, though: K is I divided by <. And now I am alone and empty, with only a few mundane chores to carry out before we can be joined, I hover near them, separated from them by thin glass. A girl comes into the red, rounded room.

She is Jane. I never saw her before like this. Was this the way Jane talked and moved? Against the sides of the swinging bulb I see Jane's life pass in flickering characters. She looks a fool there with Stephen, giggling . . . a colour that sums up a whole year of her life passes, scratched on the glass like a Chinese ideogram . . . a stone, next, that is the house where she lived as a child. And Tony. He stands, last in line of her worldly lovers, while the others, ahead of him, look at her without recognition, and jostle for a place to show off their importance. Poor Jane! She is in her own street now, which is still showing as tiny as when she was lying in bed, and she, as small as a witch's doll, is walking along it. When she turns into the garden of the block of flats, and the cuckoo spit on the already browning grass washes over her thumb-high legs, will she walk up and right into me? Yet at the same time I can still see her, in the semi-transparency of Meg's room, sitting large as life beside Gil-martin. Below me, in the room where Tony and my body lie, it is dark and stifling. There is a smell of sweating flesh. In the red room, as my shrunken figure crosses the glass, Meg is speaking in a low, intense voice, and Gil-martin nods his head but still doesn't look at me.

"You can rest assured that society will thank you, will praise you for your bravery," she is saying. "For, just as society is responsible for the creation of such monsters as Mrs Marten and Miranda, so, when it is purged of them and reconstituted, it will exonerate you of any blame for violent acts performed symbolically. You are leading the way, Jane."

I can see Jane nodding, although she looks afraid. What are they leading her into now? I wish I could break through the glass and discover how she feels. For it must be extraordinarily wonderful to be with Gil-martin like this, as close as if they met every day . . . and yet I can feel nothing, shut off out here. I'm not ready yet, I know, to find my wholeness but all the same . . . the scene in the red room is as frustrating as a romantic movie, with all those feelings nothing but dead celluloid. In my cut-off state, it's hard to imagine that I'll kill Tony's mother . . . but for Meg . . .

Jane gets up, she is ready to leave. I see that, like me, she is wearing a skirt that is too short and too tight for her. She looks like an overgrown child who has forced herself into her younger sister's clothes. Gil-martin turns in his chair and smiles at her. Meg goes to open the door. And the bulb shrinks and swings, glowing in a last, bright red as Meg and her companion turn to burning fibres once more. I am alone. I am Jane, or what remains of her. Like a heavy fish in an aquarium I float in the dark, confining room.

The room is smaller. The window has gone. Round my head, as I struggle downward to the cluster of people now obscuring the bed, are long dresses smelling of mothballs and scent, and skirts bunched on hangers, and ghostly ruched shirts. I know it is Ishbel's mother's cupboard. I can feel her in the clothes. We're hiding in the cupboard, all the children from the village, and Ishbel, and me—my annual invitation, along with the village children, to go to the big house. So it's Christmas. I remember walking along the road on the side of the hill. It wouldn't snow, although the clouds were heavy with it. I was in a best dress made of scratchy wool. And my mother stood at the gate to wave me goodbye. Her hand was the only thing that moved. There was no wind, just as there was no snow: the valleys and the sky were paralysed, the slightest tremor would bring the storm, and obliteration. And all the colours were raw. It was almost January—the place needed the snow poultice. Then some of the terrible cold would go. I walked quickly, keeping my eyes on the frozen crevices in the road. When I broke out of the valley, and the next one opened up in front of me, I would see the house, which sat there as if it had always done so, smugly, in a square garden protected by hills.

Ishbel's mother and my father gave us tea at a long table in the main hall. It was a cheap village tea, and we ate slowly and politely. The food seemed to stick in our throats. The crackers only made a sound of tearing paper. My father made a speech. He said he was glad to see us there. He must remind us again that upstairs was out of bounds for games after tea. Now he was going to put out the light and we could see the Christmas tree. He would call out our names, alphabetically.

Yes, I remember that. I am down amongst the other children now, and a very faint light from under the door shows shiny, scrubbed faces and, in the case of the girls, hair wrenched back into bows for the party at the big house. How have we disobeyed my father like this and come up into the most forbidden place of all, Ishbel's

mother's bedroom? My heart begins to race. It's my
fault. It must be. I led them here, and we'll all pay the
price for it—except for Ishbel.

The lights in the hall went out and the Christmas tree
lights went on, as they did every year. The small children
were pleased at the blue and the red and the green. I sat
looking at the big windows in the hall, which stood as
straight and bare as the branches beyond them in the garden. There was an early moon. Where did I come 'alphabetically' in the list of names this time? Some years my
father avoided the embarrassment of my namelessness by
calling me last as if I were an afterthought, or a guest, or
someone who had turned up at the party by mistake—
sometimes he got it over by summoning me first, before
the children had settled and taken in what was going on.
The girls always got dolls, the boys dinky cars. My row
of dolls from past parties stood on the top shelf of the
dresser in my mother's cottage. I never played with them.

The child next to me in the cupboard nudges me hard
in the stomach. They can all hear someone coming but
my heart is too loud for that. There's little air in here. The
breaths are sweet, a mixture of cake and bread and paste.
I think I can make out Ishbel, on the far side of the cupboard from me, leaning against the door. She looks
excited and frightened. More of her vicarious thrills! For
Ishbel will be only mildly punished for this. She came
after all from the skirts which are draped round us, and
we are from the outer ring, the squat houses which produce manpower for the big house. We have no right to
be under her mother's skirts. Downstairs her motherly

role is a farce. She would rather die than foster us.

This year my father called me last, so I had to wait with my hands sweating on my lap while the children were led up by their parents, and curtseyed or bowed and were led away again. When it was my turn to go to the tree I realised how much bigger I was than I had been the year before. And Ishbel's mother saw it too: she looked at me with hatred as she handed me the neatly wrapped package with the doll inside. I was big and awkward standing there, but she saw me as a woman no doubt, as my mother again. I was blinded for a moment by the lights from the tree and I blinked at her. She turned away abruptly. Usually there was a scatter of applause after each presentation, but now there was silence. I stumbled into the bench on the way back to my seat. The main lights went on. Now that his job was done, there was no sign of my father. I knew he had gone to his study, to take a drink.

Ishbel has edged her way through the crowd of children and is at my side at last. She looks up at me with teasing eyes. Yes, she engineered this! I remember now. We all played in the big hall, and there was some half-hearted thumping on the piano, and while the parents of the village children huddled round the fire and nervously turned down offers of cigarettes and tea, she made us climb the stairs at the far end of the hall. We had to go on hands and knees. We were on the first floor landing before we knew how we got there. And we ran down the dark passage as if we were trying to bury ourselves right in the centre of the house.

The steps are in the room now. It's my father, but there

are other men with him as well. Ishbel is so close to me we could have been sewn together. The teasing look has gone and she is worried. But there is still something triumphant about the set of her shoulders and her round, spoilt face. By standing so close to me, of course, she is both protecting and condemning me. They won't strike in our direction, for fear of hitting her. But she will point the finger at me, and I'll be marched away. My ribs are tight with fear. One of the children begins to sob. And my father pulls the cupboard door open, our side first, as I knew he would.

What I hadn't taken into account is the torch. It hits me straight between the eyes, and Ishbel too, so that she whimpers aloud and claps her hands to her face. The game isn't funny for her any more. The other children file out miserably into the room. I hear my father ordering them to go downstairs, find their parents and go home. And as Ishbel and I instinctively edge backwards from the light into the depths of the cupboard, my hand clasps a dress and brings it down round my shoulders. Now I am really caught! The dress is light, and highly scented. I am standing in the bright light in the act of stealing Ishbel's mother's dress. My father, and Ishbel, and Ishbel's mother's dress, and I. There is absolute silence. My hand flies to my neck, to disentangle myself. It comes across something hard . . . a pin, a brooch . . .

"I'm so terribly sorry to disturb," Mrs Marten said. "But I feel the most *gnawing* pains of hunger. I know you're tired after the journey, Tony dear, but . . ."

Because our room was dark—Tony had pulled the curtains together before getting into bed—Mrs Marten appeared in the door in a fantail of light, her small body thrust forward and a gin and tonic sparkling in her hand. She stared greedily at us. "Your dear friend is still here, Jane. Shall we all lunch together? I've discovered rather a sweet little Italian place round the corner."

"Oh, Mummy!" Tony was on his back with his eyes closed. "Do you really have to?"

The door opened wider. The light swelled to the shape of a bowl and began to encroach on the bed. I shrank from it, under the sheet, into the recesses of the cupboard where Ishbel still stood guilty and trembling, down to blackness. Even so, I could feel the stretching daylight on the top of the bed and round the room. When it saw me it would strip me bare. And I, white flesh and hair, crouching by the warmth of Tony under the covers, would be reduced to X-ray, gutted.

"If Jane isn't well she could have some soup here and we could go." Mrs Marten's voice was muffled, but strong. "Come, Tony, there's *nothing* in the house, you know!"

Then there was Gala. I was in the cupboard still. I heard Ishbel's mother's voice, her sharp cry of alarm when she saw her trampled dresses. I tore the pin from the thin folds of the dress that had got enmeshed around my shoulders. I fought with it, hung with the sweet-scented silk like an animal caught in a trap of leaves. I lifted the glinting pin, silver with a single bright blue eye.

"Go on," said Gala. "Now!"

"You'll come to the restaurant, I hope? I had such a

lovely cannelloni there. And, you know, there's never *anything* here!"

Oh, I don't know how I could have done it! Ishbel was looking at me suddenly with such frankness. I could have trusted her with the rest of my life. She was very close to me again, crouching on shoes in the very back of the cupboard; there were discarded dresses there, neatly bundled but worn and old: in the skirts of a black dress we squatted like sisters, hiding from our mother the enemy. Her gaze was very soft . . . very appealing! Her eyes seemed to have grown lighter, even in the gloom there, but her mouth and chin were ugly still: there was nothing she could do about that. She was quite unlike my mother. Why was she so close to me? I could feel her breath on my neck. And her shoulder looked as if it had sprouted from mine. I had to lean forward to press the pin home. Right in the middle, between her breasts that weren't yet breasts. It went in very easily, leaving the eye shining on her chest.

"Now run," Gala said.

Ishbel fell as heavily as a dropped doll when I left her side. I dived under the beam of light from the torch. My father's legs were running towards me, but I dodged them. There . . . to leave the house . . . lighter already . . . the great square house in the square garden was behind me when I was on the hill, in a total darkness. No snow. Thank God, no snow as yet.

"Perhaps I'd better book a table," Mrs Marten said. "He's a sweet man. Used to be at Da Lorenzo."

Tony's legs were moving beside me in the bed. "I'll

get up then," he said in the tone that suggests he is doing a lot of women a great favour. "What's the time?"

"Well, that's the point! It's nearly two!"

"All right, all right. Come on, Jane . . . aren't you hungry?"

Tony kicked me under the covers. In my darkness I knew Gala and Mrs Marten had left the room and closed the door. The light had gone. I saw the end of my race to my mother's cottage, but only in the dull reds and blacks of the dark room. That was all that was safe for me now. I must not be exposed. I could merge in the infrared light, a shadow, half-developed, visible one minute, gone the next. But to go out into the street . . .

Tony pulled back the covers and gave me a quick glance. He dressed quickly and efficiently, snapping into his pants and trousers as if he wished he'd never taken them off. "You look all right! You must be hungry, Jane, aren't you? Don't imagine I'm going to have lunch with Gala and my mother without you!"

It was certainly a strange party. It was true, I had to go. As always, I felt it was my fault for having Gala round there, rather than Tony's fault for having a mother like Mrs Marten. If I covered my head, stayed close to the wall . . .

Tony pulled back the curtains. I groaned again. The light pulled at the skin of my face. My eyes ached, as if the daylight would pull them out.

"You must have got a migraine," Tony said. There wasn't a trace of sympathy in his voice. He pulled the quilt up over his side of the bed, and left the room. I lay there by his pristine side of the bed and wondered if I was even there. Had he been beside me; had we made love? I looked up at the bulb on the brown flex. It swung empty over my head. I pulled down Tony's cover and stared at the sheet. His stain was there, a grey mark shaped like a fish. I pulled the cover back.

Gala called me through the door. "Get up, Jane! It'll be OK! You must eat, you see!"

They got me out with difficulty. I had to find a scarf for my head, and ended up with a black Greek scarf with gold sequins stitched on it that I had once bought on holiday in Delphi with another boyfriend—only to discover too late that the scarf denoted widowhood, death. I tied it under my chin and followed Mrs Marten and Gala and Tony out of the flat and onto the swirling lino. Mrs Marten's stiletto heels went down into the rubber with an airport sound and Tony trudged beside her: they might have been leaving, meaninglessly, for an international destination. I thought of the way they took and squandered and consumed the world, as if it had been laid out for them like a tray of hors d'oeuvres. Once, Mrs Marten would have been considered a sinner. Now she merely slimmed. I thought of Meg's instructions, in the crystal ball in my bedroom. And I could see Mrs Marten as disposable. The only sign of her non-existence would be an inscription on a board in her upholstered shrubbery: *For Sale*. It had been her motto, now it could be her epitaph.

We reached the street. How easy that sounds! Gala knew what I was suffering and hung back with me. The main door was open and Tony and his mother were passing through; I could see the patch of grass, grey of course, and by the gate the long uncut grass with the cuckoo spit, grey on grey now like an arty photograph. Beyond, the lumpy old women were walking, and a couple of grim youths in clerical 'fifties-style suits and steel-rims, conspicuous austerity. It was a brilliantly sunny day. The colourless trees cast deep shadows on the pavements. Broken glass outside Paradise Island glinted like coal in the shadows from the houses. I stood in the hall with my back to the grandiose mango wallpaper and my hands spread out on the walls by my side. How could I go out there? Had I really killed Ishbel? Or would she be waiting for me, always fleetingly behind me or ahead of me, blameless, triumphant, with a fixed smile on her lips above the stabbed heart? It was hard to believe she was gone. I had felt freer while anticipating her disappearance than I did now. Perhaps this was an omen—I would in no way benefit from the end of Miranda.

"It's only round the corner," Gala said. "Walk quickly and it'll all be over."

I went out, still holding her hand—Tony hadn't waited for us and we had to pull the door open again: it had swung shut while I hesitated. Now we passed the long grass and opened the wrought iron gate, and we were in the street. Tony and Mrs Marten were quite a way ahead: just passing the battered wives' home, in fact, and I saw Mrs Marten look up at the building and give the little wrinkle of her nose which she considered a charming and rueful expression in the face of something unacceptable.

I watched one of the women come out, with a two-year-old child in one arm and a bag of washing for the launderette in the other. She looked at Mrs Marten, in her white suit and her high white shoes and her white hair in a cascade of ringlets, as if she had just landed from the moon. Then she came along the street towards me. Her face was tired and her breasts drooped. She looked at me once, and then down at the pavement. Then she looked up at me again. Her eyes went wide. She pulled the child into her so that it wriggled at the tight grip.

"Keep walking," Gala said. She spoke in a low voice. "Don't stop!"

Why did I now feel the fear too? The woman wasn't Ishbel, after all. Or was she the first to notice that Ishbel was really dead at last? I watched her shadow approaching in ripples on the bars of the railings that guard basement steps and areas. It ran towards me, snaking on the bars, as large as a mother goddess, with the child fused into the body of the mother and the two heads rising and dipping as they came.

"Jane!"

Mrs Marten was standing outside Paradise Island now, in her 'model pose', stomach well in and head back, a tiny provocative smile on her lips. "Do hurry, dear!" Behind her a powerful woman was cleaning the windows. She looked at me with impatience. What did she see? A sad woman in a black scarf, walking nervously near the railings as if she might have to cling to them for support, a sad woman accompanied by another woman with a singular lack.

Mrs Marten saw, at the same time as the woman from the wives' home was giving vent to her anxiety by literally breaking into a run, screwing up her eyes as if the sun had suddenly become too strong, dashing past me with a sort of muttered grunt of apology. Mrs Marten dealt with the phenomenon with a good deal more elegance, as she would certainly have expected of herself in the circumstances. She took Tony's arm—he too was standing impatiently at the junction with the main road, as if Gala and I were not to be trusted in a public thoroughfare—and went graciously up on tiptoe to whisper in his ear. I saw him frown. She didn't point, of course: that would have been bad manners.

It was then that Gala and I began to laugh. I was afraid still, and the laughter ran through me like electric current. Here, in the hard, bright street with the summer leaves that looked as if they had been sprayed with silver tinsel, and the sharp white paint on the houses, and the crooked black shade, and Mrs Marten standing upright and ridiculous in her white outfit, at the end of the street, were Gala and I walking without shadows, vulnerable in the extreme, shadows ourselves, spreading terror as we went! We were invisible except for our laughter, our nervous systems, our X-ray spines. If we had no shadows we couldn't be alive. And Mrs Marten, like a figure in a cartoon, frozen with disbelief, awaited us there. Outside Paradise Island, of all places! O women who love women, take heart from us! We drove away our shadows, and look at us now!

Gala still had a hold on my arm, as if to show we would

be stronger together than apart. I felt my feet very light, I might float off the ground altogether, but not as I was when I flew at the command of Meg. I was weak, my body barely obeyed me. And now Mrs Marten was only a few feet away, with Tony at her side wearing an expression of utter incredulity. Our laughter seized us once more. What did this mother-and-son team want from us then? Respectable ladies with proper, well-dressed shadows, and bank cards in our handbags? Sorry we couldn't oblige! By the time we were at the corner of the street, the same mercury flowed in our veins. Whether we still belonged to this world or not, we would give the Martens all they deserved. And part of me marvelled at the way Gala could give me such empathy, as if the condition was hers for the first time too. Without her I might have been seized—exterminated—in the overpowering light of this day.

But the extraordinary thing was that neither Tony nor his mother referred to what they had seen. Tony nodded at us and said briskly: "Funny we never noticed this place before, Jane. I wonder how long it's been going?" He indicated the restaurant canopy, which jutted out in the main road just beyond the supermarket. And Mrs Marten, twinkling at Gala, said: "Normally it's vitamins and a salad for lunch for me. But—I don't know why—I feel so *ravenous* today! It must be the party at the Belgian Embassy last night. Do you know, the food was virtually uneatable!"

Gala and I exchanged glances. The laughter turned warm and pleasant inside us. So the Martens couldn't face the confrontation! But we knew we were in a position of power now, and it was they who were afraid at last. Who and what did they think they were going to lunch with at the trattoria? Did they sense their hour had come? Tony, even, smiled in friendly encouragement at me as we went into the clean, Italian interior. He had seen me looking at the supermarket as we passed, perhaps, and as always had misunderstood my reactions. "Look, Jane, if you've not been feeling too well in the last few days since I've been away, I'll get the shopping in this afternoon. Mummy says there's nothing in the house. I mean, I'll just get the basics, if you like!"

Eating and buying, shitting and dieting, the Martens stumbled towards their allotted places in the cemetery in the Surrey hills. That was expensive too: Tony's father was buried there and I had heard all about the cost. I shook my head, allowing myself a beatific smile. It was good, to feel the power of his fear. Mrs Marten was bending over backwards to sit Gala in the best seat at the table. She would do anything to postpone the hour of her death. Gala and I laughed again as we settled ourselves in the bright restaurant. Here, because of the bustle of people, and the moving light and shade from the low lamps which swing back and forth as customers come and go, our absence of shadows would hardly be noticeable. Perhaps that is what relieved Tony and his mother: unpleasant and embarrassing scenes could be avoided, for the moment anyway.

I WRITE THIS as the hour draws near, and in such confusion that I can't tell exactly what took place since
yesterday . . . whether I dreamed . . . or if Mrs Marten
put some drug in my wine at lunch . . . or how much I
saw or imagined. Certainly the lunch went 'ordinarily'
enough, with Tony and his mother discussing the prices
of property in Central London, and the possible dates for
shooting *Chance*, and summer holiday plans until, looking
up and across Gala, who was eating quietly with her eyes
fixed on her plate, I saw Meg sitting at a table opposite.
There was a man with her . . . it was he . . . but he had
his back to me. Meg smiled at me and waved. I stared.
Mrs Marten noticed, of course, and, ever eager for social
contacts, whipped an eyeglass from her bag. Then she
turned to me and nodded. She still held the eyeglass
aloft, and it was between Meg and me now, so that I
could see her, magnified in a third eye, still smiling and
very close. I flinched. Meg winked at me. Under the table
I found Gala's foot and kicked it hard.

"Meg Gil-martin," said Mrs Marten. "An old Scottish
family! I can't see who the man is, though!"

"Wasn't she at the Berrings' party?" said Tony.

Gala took my hand under cover of the tablecloth. I felt drained, half-alive. Between them, the Gil-martins and the Martens would crucify me, tear me from the material world into the outer regions, and back again. I saw land, I saw heaving seas, I saw a ship leaving a calm port, and a black cave in which I flapped without hope of escape. My face flamed. I looked down at my sitting body, polite by the white table, and the sun that fell in over the white tiled floor, and the hard white place where my shadow should have been. I looked up again. Meg was talking and laughing with her companion, as she had when she appeared in the glass in my bedroom. Had she come to give me moral support, to ensure that Mrs Marten would be dealt with as she ordained? I glanced from one woman to the other. Mrs Marten was preening herself in a compact mirror now, and Meg—or a slice of Meg—was reflected alongside her. Why did they seem suddenly so alike—I could hardly tell the difference! Or did I see resemblances everywhere, now that my own double was so near her end? I stared fascinated at the twin reflections —Mrs Marten was dabbing her nose—but Gala pulled at my fingers under the table and muttered to me to stop.

Some waiters went by with a trolley, and when they had passed and the space between the tables was clear again, Meg's table was empty. I heard myself gasp, and Mrs Marten's voice, from a great distance, asking what the matter was.

"Jane isn't herself," Tony said succinctly. And so the rest of the meal went by, with Gala's and my high spirits somehow dampened by the reminder of Meg, and Tony and Mrs Marten at the zenith of their powers, their imposed vision of the world, their roundness and sureness in the face of our terrifying insubstantiality all the more crushing and oppressive as the pasta and veal-in-Marsala and crisp salad and chocolate sweet came and went.

I didn't go home after that. But I don't know what I did. It seems to me that I went to see Stephen . . . Gala must have helped me to get there . . . I remember his sitting room, with the curtains drawn. I must have asked him for darkness and closed them myself, for I can still see his large, comforting figure in the armchair and the outline of his face. He didn't seem surprised. But he couldn't help me either: my force was stronger than his, and slowly I disrupted the atmosphere of mild, complacent expectation of sanctity in which he lived. We sat in silence. From the corners of the dim room a cold wind got up, and there was the sound of rustling leaves. I closed my eyes. I knew the forest had pursued me here. After a while Stephen put his head in his hands. He was beaten, and we both knew it. But his fear made me uneasy, for I felt nothing but patience and resignation, a waiting for the night.

It came at last. I left Stephen without a word and went out onto the pavement. I was strong now in the cover of night, and I had a raging hunger. I was going to the house where Miranda lived, to reconnoitre, to plan for the next day, and my other sister walked with me but she, too, would soon be taken away. I knew that and I held her close. We walked through the dark streets, which were full of people as soundless as ghosts, and soon we were in the garden of that terrible house—it was a winter evening again and bright with stars—and we went in at the back door and up the uncarpeted servants' stairs to our room. What had we done? What crime would we pay for now? There was a note pinned to my pillow. It was from the mistress of the house. It said £2 each was to be deducted from the wages of Jeanne and Marie to repair the iron broken that morning. That was all. We stood and faced each other in the narrow room with the sloping ceiling and the dead flies that accumulated every day on the window sill. In the past, my sister would have sobbed. But now we just stared into each other's eyes. Four eyes —dark—fringed with black.

It took me some time to arrive at Miranda's house. It was a house that had been converted into three flats, and I knew she lived at the top, also in rooms with attic ceilings; she would have made the flat 'sweet', though, and there would be bunches of flowers in the wallpaper. I saw her at once, outlined against the window, staring straight down at me as if offering her throat. She was pale, her eyes were black, and there was a slight smile on her lips.

Marie took the note from the pillow and scrumpled it into a ball. She was the strong one now. I had never seen such hatred in anyone. She turned to me and her eyes told me to follow her. So I went back down the stairs, but on the landing where the baize door to the bedroom floor stood closed, we stopped as if we knew that this was where we must stay. We stood there, by the door which

was there to muffle our sound. We looked down the well
of the poorly lit stairs, and we smelt the dinner for the
rich Aldridge relations. Pheasant and breadcrumbs and
green beans. We were meant to be there, handing it.
Instead we had fled across the frosty fields and tried to
escape but, as always, we were driven back by cold and
hunger and we had failed. What would they do to us,
now we hadn't turned up? My God . . . they were helping
themselves . . . we could hear chairs scraping and heavy
footsteps, and the popping of a cork.

Miranda opened the window and leaned out. She wore
a black silky top, which showed her white breasts as she
leaned towards me. I thought I could see behind her a
kitchen exactly like my own. Yes, even the white enamel
drainer was the same, hanging on a peg over the sink.
She was still smiling, but without any gaiety, as if she was
expecting me to come up and take over her kitchen there
and then. But I wouldn't! I hugged Marie to me. I wasn't
ready yet, and neither was Meg. Poor Miranda, she would
simply have to wait.

Marie and I were still very close together when the
baize door suddenly opened and Mrs Aldrige and her
daughter appeared on their part of the landing. They
must have left the dining room, come in search of us,
keener on vengeance for the broken iron and our truancy
than on their own rich food. Behind them the soft colours
of the main passage glowed, red and gold in the Persian
carpet that ran the length of the passage, orange in the
walls hung with oils of horses and loved dogs. Mrs Aldridge's scent was strong that night. I tried to step back,

pulling Marie with me. It was then I realised she wasn't going to come.

If you don't retreat, you must either stand still or go forward. I felt the pull in me as Miranda, perversely, as if she half-hoped to plunge to her death in my arms, leaned further out of the window, and Marie, unrecognisable in her strength and determination, stepped forward until she was within a few inches of our employers. Now that Miranda was poised like a swimmer about to push off from the bar, more of the kitchen was visible behind her. I saw the black and white jars, labelled 1, 2, 3, 4, in which I keep coffee and sugar and old herbs I never use. I resented her having these too! Did Tony buy two sets then, furnish two kitchens at the same time? But as I stared at the numbers on the jars, I felt my hands going up—as if I wanted to get up there, to take hold of them as my property, to unstopper them and take the contents —and my hands were on Mrs Aldridge's daughter's throat, twisting, unscrewing, squeezing the porcelain neck. Marie had pulled out her mistress's eyes! They lay on the landing, one on the rich Persian carpet and the other nearer the edge where the bare boards began. Louise! I saw her distracted gaze as I knelt on the hill with the sharp stone in my hand. My mother . . . my Marie . . . generations of cruel mothers in rich corridors fell under our blows. When they had gone we would be whole. Well, we had the women so close they couldn't make a sound, except for a choking fighting for breath that sounded like wind going through the winter branches of the trees outside.

Still, Miranda was smiling down at me. I was horrified at her. Couldn't she see what she was doing: condemning Marie to death, and therefore herself too? For I saw now for the first time that Marie had put scissors in her pocket before running down from our room—and a length of piping which she must have always had concealed on her from the beginning of the afternoon when we tried to run away. The piping was thrust into my hand. How did I follow suit and hack them to pieces like that? The blood began to flow quite freely, sinking into the carpet without any difficulty, but running thin over the wooden boards, leaving erratic stains which leapt in front of my eyes as I struggled with my prey. Oh, we were grunting by now, Marie and I. And I had the daughter's eyes out too: I threw them down the passage with a shout that brought the men running. But Marie had never been so close to me. It was my last day with her, and we were half-drowned in blood!

Miranda took herself back into her kitchen. She drew across a curtain that flowered in pink and white, quite unlike mine. I stood on the pavement beneath her window, with the streetlamp shining on me and my eyes in deep shadow, as she had once stood beneath me. But I don't know how I got home. The streets were empty then of the silent crowds—I must have walked again—and this time there was no Marie at my side.

The men found us in our room, where we had fled after my shout. There was such a smell of fresh blood in the corridors, so many hacked limbs lying there, there was almost an instinct in me to tidy it all away before I ran. But Marie grabbed me ... we stripped off our clothes ... we lay deep in the narrow bed. Then the men came and wrenched us apart. Their sobs were loud and hoarse. I knew, as they carried Marie's unmoving body from the room ahead of mine, that she would die in a prison cell far from me.

"Jane, my dear!"

Mrs Marten's voice comes through the door. It must be late, there is sun behind the curtains and Tony has got up and left for work. Someone has hung a ballerina dress of pink net with a spangled bodice on a hanger on the outside of the cupboard, and beside it my dusty jeans and jacket. What can this mean ... where did the dress come from? ... and who has been interfering with the clothes I will wear when I finally go? It's Mrs Marten, of course. This is intolerable! I spring out of bed, but the glare from the day gives me a headache and I sink back again. I can hear her stepping about in the passage, as if she's trying to make up her mind to come in.

"I do think you should have some coffee! And what do you think of the outfit?"

This gets me to the door and I pull it open with a violence that obviously surprises her because she titters and waltzes away from me in the direction of the kitchen.

"What is that dress doing in my room?" I can hear my voice still thick with exhaustion from the night. "And where did you find those jeans?"

"My dear, do they belong to a younger brother? I didn't know you had one!" Mrs Marten stands in the

194

doorway to the kitchen, arms akimbo and eyes blazing with malice. Over her arm is what appears to be a harlequin costume. One blue leg and one red dangle against her thigh. A cap with bells is suspended from the kitchen door-handle. I feel a chill . . . a terror . . . I will certainly never be able to despatch Mrs Marten into the other world! She will haunt me forever, bells ringing softly as she moves . . . divided, lozenge-patterned body thin and nimble as a cat.

"The ballerina dress belonged to my poor dear sister," says Mrs Marten. She must guess at my thoughts, for she is backing slowly into the kitchen as she speaks. In my panic I know Tony is miles away: she may have sent him away forever. I must be on my guard now, for it's a battle to the end between us. Yet I have never felt clumsier, less alert.

"I just felt I would love you to wear it, you see! Do, Jane—it would make me so happy to see her again in you. She was quite promising as a ballet dancer, you know— but then grew a teeny bit too tall. And then . . . I thought I'd told you all this before but sometimes, you know, one is too upset to talk about these things . . . she died. Mummy and I were . . ."

I walked along the passage, monstrous in size compared to her. My nightdress sucked at my heels. "I'm sorry to hear that," I said. "What did she die of?"

"Too tragic. Leukaemia. It often takes the young and gifted, I fear! So, Jane, will you? But I'm being too awful when you haven't had your coffee yet. Look, I've got it ready for you!"

I'm at the kitchen door. I reach for the handle, but the

little jester's cap repels me. I step in. My kitchen is less familiar to me than Miranda's. Is it just that I can no longer stand the light? Even the white enamel strainer on the peg by the window looks somehow like a copy of the original. But there's something else . . .

"It may seem banal to you that I should want to go as Pierrot! But do you know it's always been a dream of mine . . . ever since I was a child."

Now Meg's voice begins to sound in my head. The rosy glow, which always intensifies when she comes to me, dots the strainer over with red and makes a sunset on the white lino floor. I take another step forward.

"She's Mrs Aldridge, Jane! Think of your and Marie's bravery last night! And think of the great deed that lies ahead. But first, Jane, before she destroys you . . . take her . . . with the knife!"

"I must say I'm rather grateful to have been invited to this do!" (Why is Mrs Marten apparently intentionally leading me on, drawing me further and further into the kitchen, she is almost by the window now, where Miranda leaned out so perilously last night.) "I spoke to Miranda this morning and she said she'd been invited too. She says she knows the film director *very* well . . . she's known him for years. It's extraordinary how many people Miranda knows, don't you think, Jane?"

I'm sure I've never seen this knife before. It's smart and has a French name on the handle. Did Mrs Marten buy it for the purpose? Will she spring forward, wrench it from my grasp?

"Jane, do you want to cut some bread with that knife?

If so, I've moved the bread over here, near the window. I thought the bin was in *such* a fusty place! And that's when I came across that rather dirty pair of jeans, and jacket. I hope you don't mind me popping them in your room, but I thought if you looked at them you'd be bound to decide to give them to Oxfam, or something!"

Mrs Marten has become quite breathless. I am advancing on her, which she seems to have willed, but as I walk I feel my feet drag on the floor, and a wave of faintness come over me. Oh, not now . . . the faintness takes part of my vision, so that I see only segments of the room, and the window, and small chips of Mrs Marten like a mosaic with missing pieces. I can feel my legs give, and bring me down to the floor . . .

"Jane, I *told* Tony you weren't well. I think we should call the doctor! I don't think you should go to the party at all!"

Meg, where are you now? I lie on the floor and stare up at the ceiling. I begin to choke. The white bulbs hang together as thickly as fungus growing on a tree. They are hung on wires, and the wires are nailed in to the corners of the ceiling. They are round and white, but their skin is flaky, like paper. My mouth opens, but I can't even retch. And as I lose consciousness I know Mrs Marten can't have fixed them up there on her own. So Tony helped her! They know how to make me disappear! My eyes close, as the bulbs swell, and come down on me . . .

I am in bed. So I'm ill. It must be late afternoon, the light is comfortable to the eyes, but how weak I have become!

Did Meg know the battles I would have to survive in this world before she let me into the other? Crash! There go the soft drink crates outside Paradise Island . . . it must be even later than I thought . . . it's strange, but now I can't see the street and the trees that are dead to my eyes, and the generations of women on the pavement, I miss it . . . I don't really want to leave. I'm afraid of catching Miranda, and going to the new regions. Suppose I could become a part of this street and walk every day to the supermarket and dance with the women at Paradise Island, and talk to the bruised women, and grow old with the women with their parcelled bodies, wouldn't it be better, more accepting than what I have in store? But Meg tells me I will never suffer. I'm sanctioned, so she would have me believe.

I look round the room. Certainly they're treating me like an invalid! Stephen is sitting in a chair at the end of the bed, and Gala is cross-legged on the floor near the window. Am I as ill as all that? They've brought grapes, and bunches of sweet peas and roses. The sweet peas are right by my bed, on the low table where Miranda's photograph once lay. They look like moth's wings, only in the colours of an early sky. I don't like them . . . I try to move the jug, but my hand is trembling and misses it altogether. Stephen is smiling reassuringly at me. Am I going to die then? What have Tony and his mother done?

"Where's Tony?" I say. "And . . . what time is it?"

"It's six," Gala says. "Tony'll be back in a minute, won't he?"

"What happened to me? Am I ill?"

"Mrs . . . Mrs Marten rang *me*," Stephen says. "She said you were ill. And Gala too I suppose . . . what did she say to you, Gala?"

Thank God, they can understand my anxiety. Has Mrs Marten formed a plan to stop me from going to the party? She suspects, perhaps, that I was going to follow Miranda from room to room and—how clever!—she's pinned me here with my friends instead.

"She said she'd been worried for some time," Gala says. "Had been particularly worried at our lunch!" At this, Gala burst out laughing and I tried to smile—but the vile substance from the kitchen was still in my mouth and to move my lips was painful.

"She even went so far as to suggest that you had a disease her younger sister died of . . ."

"Yes," Stephen puts in. "She told me the doctors thought you had leukaemia."

"But it's unbelievable . . ." I struggle to sit upright. Now I see that both Stephen and Gala are looking very upset. Am I so pale, then? Is Mrs Marten going to finish me off so easily?

The door opens. Tony comes in. The draught from the opening door ruffles the curtains and, as they blow apart, for an instant I see the grey leaves on the top branches of a tree and a new moon, cruelly small and thin, hanging in the sky. The parrot gives a long whistle. Tony is followed by his mother—of course: I stare at Gala and Stephen, willing them to stay, dreading that they will go now or just disappear into the ether.

"I agree we should get the doctor," Tony is saying to

Mrs Marten. "If we can get him to come quickly . . ." He leaves the sentence unfinished. What he means is he can get the doctor's visit over and still make the party. Tony wouldn't like it very much if he had to give that up while sitting here with me! And what would he tell Miranda, waiting in her black dress for him to come?

"We can stay with Jane and wait for the doctor," Gala says quickly. She knows, I'm sure, that she can make me better in time to get there myself. She'll get Meg over—anything.

"Oh I don't think it would be right for the family to leave Jane!" Mrs Marten says, and gives a low laugh that is supposed to be self-deprecating and compassionate. Instead, there is the chill of terror in the room again. Tony catches his mother's eye and nods.

"Luckily, I prepared rather a delicious meal," says Mrs Marten. "And of course if Jane shows improvement we could probably leave her for a minute and pop off to the party. It's your favourite, Tony darling!"

"What's that?" Tony has settled himself on the end of the bed in a husbandly way. I know he dislikes Stephen as well as Gala, and he keeps his eyes carefully away from both of them.

"Why, lobster with aioli, of course! Don't you remember when we went to Avignon and you ate *so* much of it you were nearly sick!"

"Hmm," Tony says. (Yet I know he must have hung the garlic there, that it was really all for me.) "Well, Mummy, it sounds delicious!"

"Gala, would you like to come in the kitchen and see the little feast I've prepared?"

What extraordinary behaviour! In all my weakness I can only gasp at Mrs Marten's cool insolence. But Gala knows only too well what would happen to her, even though I haven't had a chance to describe the wicked bulbs suspended from the ceiling. She shakes her head.

"I'd rather stay here with Jane, if you don't mind."

"I expect you would!" Mrs Marten gives her venomous laugh. But she seems too much in control of the situation. Where has she found her new power? She stands a moment longer in my room, with the Pierrot costume still swinging on her arm. Tony switches on the lamp, from which I recoil—she has never seemed so white, from her hair, to the dead whiteness of her face, and the white chiffon at her throat and the neat little suit and white shoes. Her eyes look out from sockets dark with eyeliner and mascara.

"I'll go and ring the doctor now, Tony dear! And then we'll eat. See you in a moment!"

There are so many people on the stairs. It's strange how the women are dressed: about half of them are witches and have black robes and pointed hats—some of them have even stuck on big, curved noses and their eyes are bright—and the others are courtesans, seductive and tempting, with beauty spots on their breasts and flounced, pretty skirts. When they look at me they smile openly. But I press on, waiting patiently to get to the top. There I will find Miranda. Every minute my strength returns.

Stephen tried to stop me from coming. He told me I should go with him, and he would help me to find Life. He had a handkerchief he kept taking from his pocket. He mopped his face with it. It's true it was oppressive in there, with the curtains still closed and the evening sounds coming in from the hot street. Every few minutes he put it back in his pocket and pushed it down before pulling it out again. Gala told me I must go. I lay listening to them, still very weak—Tony had muttered an excuse and gone to help Mrs Marten with the presentation of the aioli in the kitchen—and at one point I could have sworn Gil-martin came and joined my friends in that room, sitting on the end of the bed where Tony had sat and looking straight into my face. Yet I still couldn't describe him, if I tried: I only know I was relieved and happy to see him there, and promised I would pay no attention to anyone who tried to prevent me from carrying out my task. I would be with him later that night. I would find him when it was time.

The doctor came, a doctor I had never seen before. He said I was tired. I remember the syringe he held up to the light, and Gala knocking it from his hand. He left after an angry consultation with Mrs Marten and Tony in the passage. Then Tony came in and said supper was ready. I said I had to get dressed and they all left the room except Gala. That was how we escaped—but look at me now!

All my clothes had gone from the cupboard. Mrs Marten must have taken them. All she had left me were the jeans and the jacket, and the ballerina dress: the tulle skirt was pink, and bulged out into the room from the tin hanger, on the bodice was an assortment of tarnished sequins. And of course the jeans won't fit me till later, I'm on Miles Alton's staircase in the ballet dress and that's why people smile. It's none of me, as they say. They must imagine it's some buried fantasy of mine! But I don't care. I look up and down the staircase; some of the women are in masks; there are even one or two Pierrettes, holding the little cat-grinning faces in front of their own. None of them is Miranda, I think. If only they would go up faster! Some of the men, who know me slightly, are laughing at me openly now, and my mood of defiance won't last. Gala is beside me, as always, and a stair higher up. She is pushing with her shoulders and her face is set.

We left the flat so easily it amazes me they hadn't thought we might run when we had the chance. Stephen is too greedy—he was exclaiming with pleasure at the scarlet lobster and the great bowl of pounded garlic paste. Tony was being ordered by Mrs Marten to try and find 'good knives and forks, if such a thing exists in poor Jane's flat', and was bustling to bring up chairs. Their sense of politeness and taste and good living let us get away into the night in search of our prey! It will always be possible, in the end, to defeat such people, because if you choose the middle of dinner their defences will be down. We simply went down the main stairs and out onto the lino of the hall. I was carrying the jeans in a bag. We shut the main door and went out of the gate into the street. It was a dark evening. The new moon had gone higher up into the sky. We looked back once and there, sure enough, were the three of them in my kitchen window, smiling at each other rapturously. Gala had put her coat over my shoulders so that no one in the street, at least, could stare at my outfit. This time . . . it was the very last time . . . I knew I would never come back.

When we get to the top of the stairs I see that all the rooms have been draped with material, as if Miles Alton is trying to persuade people they're in the Arabian Nights. There are some real Arabs in evidence, no doubt he has his eye on them to put money into his films, and some stupid young English journalists wearing Arab head-dresses. On either side of Miles, who has long golden hair, two chins and a stomach gently pregnant in a striped caftan, stand a 'beautiful lady', thoroughly enjoying herself in her period costume, which pushes her breasts forward and makes it possible for her to wink and flirt behind a fan, and a tall, raven-haired witch with a false nose and a mouth under it as thin and red as a gash. What happened to women, that they were forced into these moulds? At least there are no 'wives' here, that would be too boring for a fancy dress ball! Unless . . . I grab hold of Gala's arm. At the far end of the room where we're now standing I see a figure in grey chiffon flitting about in front of a large candelabra. Her hair is dark. She is quiet and grey as a moth. I think she has a mask on, but at this distance it's difficult to tell. Surely . . . only Miranda, the rightful wife of Tony, the quiet, dark wife, would present herself at this gaudy occasion in such a way. Yet of course I had envisaged her in quite another way! Scheming, anxious to 'make' it in the film world, willing even to be taken up by a rich Arab and have money to spend. Why should I suddenly be convinced that this was she? Ah, Miranda . . . she changes and dissolves as I do . . . and as my force comes back to me now, fed by the night and the hunger that is beginning to return, she melts into softness, a wedding ring, a veil.

Gala is nodding at me in response. She says we must go in search of Miranda. We begin to push our way through the crowded room. Some film critic in lemon shorts and a tank top comes up to me and asks why I wasn't at the showing of the Francesco Rosi this morning. How hot it is in here! The incense is too strong, the heavy sweet smell of dope is rising above it and there are broken clouds of smoke on the ceiling, on the loosely hung, theatrical material which comes down in a clumsy swag in the middle of the room like a tent. There are arum lilies. Why are there so many mirrors, enclosed in swirls of bright gold, all the length of the room? I can see the reflections of the fancifully dressed, faded as ghosts in the antique glass. Some of the people are already lying on cushions the size of small boats. And suppose it isn't Miranda, or I fail, as I failed with Mrs Marten earlier on. What will be my fate then?

"About power, as all his movies are," says the film critic. "I thought you'd be there, actually."

I grin at him—he is too polite to make reference to my ridiculous *tutu*—and press on, pulled by Gala. I look round once. Horror! There is Mrs Marten already, prancing in her Pierrot costume in front of Miles Alton at the door. The little gold bells on her cap are jigging with her. I can see three of her, positioned as she is within the loom of three mirrors. In each she grimaces and gesticulates and turns her head wildly, as if searching, like me, for someone in the room. Stephen is behind her. He must have gone home in order to dress up in purple ecumenical robes: it seems strange that he should parody his faith in this way. And Tony, of course, has made no concession at all. But he looks just as irritating in his suede jacket and white polo neck as the other guests in their wild gear.

"Come on! If you go on looking at them you'll lose her for good!"

Gala is right. And now I find, as I reach the far end of the room by the big candelabra, that she has disappeared too, losing faith in me perhaps as I stood gaping in fear at Mrs Marten and her son and my friend hung with his gold crucifix. Gala is nowhere to be seen. I know none of the people standing round me. There seems to be a preponderance of beauty patches, and a scarcity of witches. One of the men had decided to come as a vampire: he has fangs of white card down to his chin, and strokes of black eye pencil on his face to suggest wickedness. He looks at me and then quickly away, as all the men do when they see the obscenity of my ballerina dress. If he could know... My mouth, which had been dried, revolted, by the horrors of the garlic in the flat, is rosy and juicy inside as freshly killed beef and my teeth, which will be so urgently needed tonight, are beginning to grow. They ache slightly, but not painfully, as they descend over my lower teeth into my jaw. How am I to find her? It must be soon.

Yet this end of the room seems to be a dead end. The walls are covered with plum silk and oil paintings of men in breeches and long coats.

One more glance over my shoulder. A waiter passes and I nearly knock him over. I take a glass of champagne. I can see Mrs Marten making her way towards me. Her white face looks more of a mask than the real ones, some of which are on sticks, as I dreamed, and waving animatedly in their owners' hands. Her face is blind and intent and terrible. A smile is set on it. She is threading her way through the crowd, horrifying in her harlequin suit. I back up against the wall at the end of the room . . . my glass swills round and the champagne spits out on the ground . . . three beauties turn their backs.

It's then that I see the hairline crack in the plum silk, neat as an incision and following the contours of a low door, but where . . . without daring to turn and face the wall I seek the handle under a long picture of a lady in a crinoline dress. There . . . my hands are sweating so that they slip from it as soon as it is found. A protuberance of metal on the silk . . . my fingers close over it again, and twist and push.

Mrs Marten is nearly on me. First a red leg and then a blue prances forward, like an illusionary army. Some way behind, I see Stephen's face, very flushed over his purple robe. There is no sign of Tony. I duck down under the picture and go backwards, half on my back, through the hidden door. I land on my bottom, on a parquet floor, and kick the door shut with my ballet-slippered foot. I crawl forward, see the gold bolt on the door and pull it across.

There! She can't get me now! But someone must have slid the bolt the other way to let me in here at all.

The room is just as I imagined it would be. It is small and square, and empty except for two small tapestry settees and a tall mirror framed with antlers of gold. The curtains are dark velvet and are tightly drawn although it is a summer night. There are candles, in a glass chandelier. And Miranda is standing in front of the mirror quietly contemplating herself. Her dress is grey and fragile. Her eyes are grey. She has added a Spanish comb to her dark hair now: it is studded with moonstones which are too dim to shine much in the light from the candles. Her expression is serious. Has she seen Tony yet? Or did they plan to meet in here? Was it for him that the door was left unbolted? What a disappointment for her that I should come instead!

I come up behind her. Did she ever keep a photograph of me? Does she know, secretly, what *I* look like? Or will she guess at once, and turn as if she's been struck in the back?

But she can't see me. I'm not there! I stand so close to her now that the slightest movement of my hand would touch her back . . . I look up and into the mirror . . . my terrible absence is there in the glass, which shows the trim settees and the bottom half of the chandelier with the candles burning fierce and upright without a flicker. My non-existence there is almost concrete . . . unreflected I feel heavier, as abandoned as a new corpse. My limbs are paralysed. I keep on staring at her. Her eyes are dim as the moonstones in her hair. And though neither of us can see me she senses me there. Her mouth opens to call out in fear.

I close in on her . . . My teeth go into her smooth neck. Miranda . . . these are my hours . . . when it's so dark outside that I can fly the streets without dread of the stake, ravenous, insatiable! You knew I was coming! You welcomed me almost. You give me your blood!

It was strange to hold Miranda in my arms like that, while Tony and his mother battered on the door behind the picture, and Stephen called to me to come out in the name of God. The blood gushed from her neck like a spring. As I drank she paled. And when the grey irises of her eyes went up into the whites and she fell backwards into my arms, I knew she was ready to take to Meg. I knew, too, how I could escape the room without going back the way I came. I pulled open the velvet curtain nearest to me, pushed up the window with one hand, and stepped out onto the parapet. There were iron stairs, just like the fire escape at home. And Gala was waiting at the foot of the stairs, with a black cab. How easy it was! I carried Miranda down without difficulty, and together Gala and I laid her on the back seat. We sat facing her on the way to Meg's, in the bucket seats.

As we travelled I looked at Miranda, and I saw the cupboard and Ishbel, and the stairs and Marie, and I saw the small, square room fill suddenly with hiding children, and the iron stairs of the fire escape, which dripped with Miranda's blood, turn to the wooden stairs in the servants' quarters of the mansion. I saw myself, in Mrs Marten's sister's ballet dress, sisterless now and ready to go. Poor Miranda! I felt sorry for her. In her own way she enjoyed life, and she made Tony happy. But in the end I was the more important of the two.

And now . . . after taking her to the red house . . . Meg delighted with me . . . I've changed to my other clothes and I walk or fly to the port. I can see the green glow from the port long before I arrive there . . . and for sentimentality's sake I take the route past the hoardings and the supermarket in the main street at the end of my road. Yes . . . as I go past so much higher than they, I see the women crowding into Paradise Island . . . husbands hanging about outside the home . . . cardboard cut-out women holding their painted Lil-lets aloft in the sodium glare. I don't look back at the flat where I live, or the glowing rooms of the Persian students opposite . . . I'm pulled by the moon, although it's small and new.

There are the sailors, there is the ship. The gangway is down. I go straight on board. And as soon as I'm there we begin our voyage. There is music, and the green lights are reflected in the oily sea.

We go out into a night that is quite black and starless, with even the moon gone. I think of Meg, as I strain my eyes in the darkness. She was so happy! I gave her what she needed! I turn to go down into the ship. But they've put the lights out here too. And that's best for me . . . for in the absence of the light I can begin to see him . . . I know he is there . . . as we sail on, with the music silenced and the waves hardly more audible than the sighing of grass on a hill, I see him standing there, by my mother's cottage on the hill . . .

Gil-martin comes towards me. The ship sails through the deep folds of the hills. I knew he would be there waiting for me!

THE END

EDITOR'S NOTE

A FEW WEEKS after reading this 'journal', some interesting new discoveries were made as to the whereabouts of Jane. In the interim, however, I had shown the document to the chief psychiatrist at the ——— hospital in London, and he and his colleagues prepared the following report. If the new discoveries seem to go rather against the findings printed here, the latter may still be of some worth to students.

Psychiatrists' Report
Jane is a schizophrenic with paranoid delusions. She is an example of the narrow border-line between depth psychology and occultism: in her case the alternation of the rational and the irrational is particularly stressed by the introduction of the supernatural. There are clearly acute problems of sexual identity, but we would suggest that there were never any such people as 'Meg' or 'K' 'Gil-martin', and that these are projections of the patient's lover Tony Marten and his mother Mrs Marten, who were unsatisfactory in their relationships

with the patient, and therefore appeared to be threatening. 'Jane's' mother seems an example of the schizogenic mother, on the one hand encouraging belligerence and independence in her daughter, and on the other demanding her attention and care.

So how are we to sum all this up? The psychiatrists went on at some length about the nature of Jane's illness—I have omitted to print this as I feel the combination of the recent discoveries, with the fact the psychiatrists showed little interest in the 'political' factor involved in her conversion (or coercion), largely invalidates the report. Is she a victim of the modern resurgence of the desire for the old magic of wholeness, for unified sensibilities? Is she really an example, as some women would have it now, of the inherent 'splitness' of women, a condition passed on from divided mother to divided daughter until such day as they regain their vanished power? As the reader will have gauged, this is not my territory, though as a field of study it appears to be expanding fast. I can only marvel at the cleverness of Margaret, or Meg, who appears, to borrow the words of a friend of mine to whom I recently showed the journal, to have "used Freud and Jung to achieve the aims of Marx". (In the event, of course, she lost out, and the Dalzell fortune is now in the hands of a second cousin, another Michael Dalzell. I sometimes wonder even, if Stephen was correct in his conjecture that it was the money only that she was after, but it does seem the most likely motive.) The odd fact that there is no mention of the killing of the father must keep the identity of Jane as his killer uncertain; but I am now more of the opinion of Stephen than I was: that a state of hypnotism prevented her from remembering that evening in March, 1976.

After my failure to find Stephen, subsequent to reading the 'journal'—and on my trip to London in July I made exhaustive and unrewarded enquiries in the Notting Hill area as to the existence of a community of women by the name of Wild, I returned north convinced that if only I could find Jane and Meg (Gala too was untraceable: it seemed she had left shortly before for Egypt and had no plans to come back) I would be able to solve the crimes and demonstrate to the public the increasing dangers of fanaticism. But when, three weeks ago, I saw the following announcement in the *Scotsman*, Thursday, September 4th, 1986, I sensed that my searches might well have come to an end. It ran as follows:

'Disturbances' Reported Above St Mary's Loch
'Strange noises and intense gusts of cold air at irregular intervals' were reported yesterday by men employed in the investigative drilling of ——— Law (formerly part of the Dalzell estate, now Government property) above St Mary's Loch. The drilling is one of several in the area for a suitable site for the burial of plutonium, the Cheviots having now received the maximum quota under safety regulations. The 'disturbances', which caused men to down tools at midday—some say they won't return to work until the area has been thoroughly

searched—seemed to emanate mainly from a circular clearing in the remains of the old Ettrick Forest. Conservationists had put forward a plea (unsuccessfully) that these ancient birches should be spared the axe, and it seems that it was at the felling of the first tree that these noises—'wailing, shouting' and cold air prevented the workmen from going any further. There had, according to Mr B. Elliot of Tibbieshiels, been some kind of a history connected with the place, and the clearing was thought locally to be haunted. The origin of the haunting is considered to be a young woman who had come to the village one night in the late 1970s, asking for bed and board. She was clearly tired and agitated, and was covered in mud. Although she had no money on her the proprietor gave her a room at St Mary's Arms. When he went up to the room in the morning she had disappeared. A child in the village saw her heading for the hills towards the old birches. Ever since, there has been fear and distrust of the clearing, although it was very infrequently visited, of course, being very high in the hills. All those who had seen the young woman said there was 'something funny' about her, and some described her as 'like a walking corpse'. However that may be, the Ministry intends to continue drilling on the site on Monday.

Two days later, on the Saturday, I was walking up the steep hill above St Mary's Loch with the Mr B. Elliot mentioned in the newspaper report. He refused any remuneration, and when I said I knew probable relatives of the deceased he became very sympathetic, and after his wife had packed up some sandwiches for us we set off.

It would be hard for me to describe the effect that lonely walk had on me after all the long months of searching for my quarry. The purple heather, which gave off puffs of a dusty pollen as we went along, and the rather dark, low clouds which were occasionally broken by an early autumnal sun, seemed all the more dramatic for being concentrated on what was formerly the Dalzell estate. Mr Elliot wasn't much of a talker, and after he'd told me he hadn't even seen the girl who, ten years before, had come in such a wild state to the village, we walked on in silence.

The clearing was right on the edge of a young pine forest, which the Forestry Commission must have planted within the last ten years. On the other side, though, was a great stretch of moor—on a clear day you might be able to see as far as Peebles—and a circle of ancient silver birches, probable remains of the Forest of Ettrick. One of the biggest trees had been felled, and there was a strong smell of the sawdust in the damp air. Some instinct led me to the far side of the clearing where the men had been too frightened to penetrate, evidently, for the fine green grass, so unnatural an occurrence in rough heather terrain, was untrampled; and there, hardly discernible in the uneven ground, was the long mound I had been half-hoping and half-dreading to find. The only sign that some hand had sculpted the mound rather than the shifting earth was the presence of a stick, a simple ash such as shepherds use, driven deep into the hardly noticeable protuberance. I

motioned to Mr Elliot—I had asked him to bring a
spade—who came over to my side and, after throwing me
a quick, perplexed glance (I think he knew, too, what
kind of thing we would find there), we started to dig.
Below us, on the outskirts of the man-made forest, was
the drilling machinery, out of use now at the weekend.
There was a good deal of sphagnum moss growing on the
mound, and the stubborn roots of heather, before we
could get down to the soil.

The first surprise was to discover that the stick wasn't,
as would normally be supposed, at the head of the grave.
It appeared to go right through the centre of the body
which, as we lifted it carefully from the shallow trough,
was in good condition still and was clothed, strangely, in
blue denim trousers and a pink top, strapless, such as
ballet dancers wear. The stick—or stake I suppose one
might call it—had pierced the body just above the ribs on
the left hand side.

We laid the body on the heather, and stood back to see
it better. I must say, I felt a strong discomfort in the air
which I think came from that unease experienced in the
face of a sudden realisation of the uncanny in ordinary
people—amongst whom I count myself, of course. There
was no way (and the uncertainty was not caused by the
results of decomposition) in which it was possible to tell
the sex of the corpse. There was something completely
hermaphroditic about it, but I can't explain what that
quality was. The face was completely blank and smooth,
and the eyes were closed. A small bosom seemed to be
discernible under the pink top, but the shoulders and

upper arms, although small, were muscular. The hair added to the anomalies of the body. It was black for about three inches—it had grown that length in the grave, I suppose—and yellow for another three, suggesting the wearer, at the time of death, had had extremely short dyed blonde hair. As all these facts tallied with the facts in the 'journal', I began to grow excited. I said nothing to Mr Elliot, of course, other than I thought this person was almost certainly the missing relative of these friends of mine and that I would apply directly for permission for the body to be moved to a morgue where they might identify it.

We replaced the body in the ground with care, and covered it with the earth again, in the event of rain. Then we went back down to Tibbieshiels to phone the police and report the discovery of the body. On reaching base, we realised that our sandwiches were still uneaten. I think Mr Elliot had been shaken by the apparition, as I had been. I thanked him, and drove back to Edinburgh.

It was only when I was safely in my flat that the significance of the stake through the body came to me. Jane had surely not done this to herself. I am in no way psychic or superstitious, but the suggestion of my psychiatrist friends, that there had never been any such people as Meg or Gil-martin (I knew better than they on the first score, anyway, as Meg must certainly have been Margaret), seemed to me more than inadequate. I was forced to wonder: if Meg did indeed have these powers, had she perhaps summoned up a certain personage, well known in the Ettrick area for many hundreds of years, called Gil-martin, who, if I remember, had plagued a young man in the seventeenth century, and whose memoirs were discovered by James Hogg. Once she had called him up, to give her the powers she needed to coerce Jane, he had become too strong for her. And he had claimed another soul . . . But these were of course the over-tired and agitated wanderings of my mind after the drama of the day on the hill above St Mary's Loch. Some passing shepherd had thrust the stick into the mound, unaware of what was beneath. I decided to make an early night of it, and went to bed.

By Monday the body had been identified by Mr Tony Marten and his mother, and 'Jane' was lying in Selkirk morgue. I went to see her frequently, with the kind co-operation of the police. Although they listened with some show of interest to my tentative theories on the long-unsolved Dalzell murders, I believe they were more intrigued by the TV programme which I would shortly be presenting and in which they would appear.

I am now practically convinced that Jane Wild killed Michael Dalzell and his daughter. But it seems I will never furnish enough proof. For a time I was so taken in by Jane's jealous descriptions of Miranda as her boy-friend's past love that I felt the woman who had written this could in no way have been describing her half-sister. The psychiatrists say, though, that this type of trans-ference is perfectly common in such cases.

There is nothing further to report, except that I went south last weekend, three weeks after the discovery of the grave, to discuss the programme and I decided to ask Tony Marten for an interview. He has of course been interviewed many times on this subject. He is now forty-five, and lives with his mother in Surrey. With some weariness he agreed to my going down to see him. Only one coincidence—and one finds plenty of those in this type of research—came up, and this was supplied by Mrs Marten, whose mind is beginning to wander, I think. I was talking of the discovery of Jane's body in the borders, and she gave a little laugh and an odd look. "Yes, poor Jane wasn't terribly well. She'd spoken to me sometimes of her love for the Scottish hills, you know, and in the end it was me who had to get her a ticket and a sleeper north. She seemed to have become quite incapable of managing things, you know!"

I could get nothing more out of her. Neither the date, nor the circumstances of the visit. Perhaps by then I was becoming superstitious and irrational myself. But as I turned to leave, she came with me to the gate and waved goodbye. She was wearing a small white petal hat, and as it was windy outside, the petals ruffled in the breeze. I don't know why, but I couldn't help remembering Stephen's description of his visit to Meg, and the white petals blowing in from the window onto her hair.

Edinburgh, October 21st, 1986